A Selection of Recent Titles from Rosie Harris

LOVE AGAINST ALL ODDS
SING FOR YOUR SUPPER
WAITING FOR LOVE
LOVE CHANGES EVERYTHING
A DREAM OF LOVE
A LOVE LIKE OURS
THE QUALITY OF LOVE
WHISPERS OF LOVE
AMBITIOUS LOVE
THE PRICE OF LOVE
A BRIGHTER DAWN

HELL HATH NO FURY

Rosie Harris

This first world edition published 2013
in Great Britain and in the USA by
SEVERN HOUSE PUBLISHERS LTD of
19 Cedar Road, Sutton, Surrey, England, SM2 5DA.
Trade paperback edition first published
in Great Britain and the USA 2013 by
SEVERN HOUSE PUBLISHERS LTD.

RE COUNCIL
LIBRARIES

British Library Cataloguing in Publication Data

Harris, Rosie, 1925-

HJ374326	
Askews & Holts	06-Jun-2014
AF	£11.99
GEN	AV

Hell ha...
1. Murder–Investigation–Fiction. 2. Romantic suspense
novels.
I. Title
823.9'...

ISBN-13: 978-0-7278-8270-7 (cased)
ISBN-13: 978-1-84751-476-9 (trade paper)

All Severn House titles are printed on acid-free paper.

Severn House Publishers support the Forest Stewardship Council [FSC], the
leading international forest certification organisation. All our titles that are printed
on Greenpeace-approved FSC-certified paper carry the FSC logo.

Typeset by Palimpsest Book Production Ltd.,
Falkirk, Stirlingshire, Scotland.
Printed and bound in Great Britain by
TJ International Ltd., Padstow, Cornwall.

For Mike O'Neill

ACKNOWLEDGEMENTS

With many thanks to Kate Lyall Grant and her wonderful team, especially Rachel Simpson Hutchens, at Severn House for all their help.

Also to my agent Caroline Sheldon and to Robert Harris for keeping my web page up to date.

ONE

Maureen Flynn suddenly felt nervous. She stared down into the liquid darkness of the coffee the waiter had just placed in front of her, and waited uneasily for her companion's next words.

Of average height, she was slim, almost anorexic by some people's standards. Her dark-grey suit and pristine white blouse had an off-the-peg look about them as if they had been chosen for their serviceability rather than style. Her straight, dark-brown hair was drawn back from her face in a French pleat, and this emphasized her high cheekbones and dark eyes. She wore the minimum of make-up, and her only item of jewellery was a gold wristwatch.

She'd been working as a freelance research assistant exclusively for Philip Harmer for the last six months, and with each passing day she had grown increasingly aware of the empathy developing between them. It was a wonderfully satisfying feeling; one that lifted her spirits so that life suddenly had a fresh sense of purpose.

Normally, Maureen ensured that her relationship with clients was on a strictly business basis, but with Philip Harmer it had been different. For her, at any rate.

She'd felt an instant affinity with Professor Harmer the very first time they'd met. He was the sort of man she admired: well-bred, well-mannered, courteous and extremely intellectual. An added bonus was that he seemed to value her opinion.

The friendship that had slowly developed between them was as fragile as fine china, and she was fearful that one of them was about to say or do something that would shatter it into a myriad of tiny pieces.

Philip Harmer was in his early fifties; thin, with aesthetic features and deep-set keen blue eyes. Some would regard him as staid since he was as conservative in his outlook as in his dress. Maureen didn't.

For her, Philip Harmer's analytical mind and powers of discernment were part of his attraction. She found that most men of her generation who held positions of authority were self-opinionated and brash. He didn't need to be pompous or egotistical. He radiated intelligence.

Professor Philip Harmer was an authority on Far East Business Development and was currently engaged in a project for one of the world's leading communication enterprises.

It was a company she had worked for many times as a freelance researcher, and they had advised him to use her services to help collate the data he required.

She had enjoyed every moment of their collaboration. Her quick probing mind complemented his attention to detail. Together they made a formidable team.

They were both workaholics. Once they discovered that neither of them had any family obligations, and very few social commitments, time ceased to exist. When they were involved in a problem they went on working as long as was necessary, until every detail had been dealt with to their complete satisfaction.

Afterwards, he would invite her to go for a drink or a meal, and as they analysed and enthused over what they had achieved she would feel a warm glow of contentment. It was a physical response unlike anything she had experienced prior to meeting him.

She had never before felt so completely at ease, or so perfectly in unison with another person. Her feelings for him deepened as the weeks working together lengthened into months.

Frequently, when they were apart, she found herself thinking about Philip. Emotional fantasies constantly filled her thoughts. There was such a tremendous affinity between them, and she felt so relaxed and safe in his company that eventually she had to admit to herself that she was falling in love with him.

It was an intellectual attraction, not a mere physical one, and this was of paramount importance to her.

She agonized about Philip's feelings for her. Did he feel

attracted towards her? Did he see her as a woman, she wondered, or merely as a skilled researcher . . . a human computer?

Her neat but nondescript appearance was a shell to hide her vulnerability. No one would believe it possible that, behind the organized efficiency she displayed in her working life, she was a quivering mass of nerves, or that she was unbearably shy. Meeting new clients filled her with unease until she became so absorbed in the work she was undertaking for them that her brain took over and her inhibitions receded into the back of her mind.

Work was her salvation, the one thing she excelled at. Immersed in the intricacies of research she was able to forget what other people might be thinking of her, forget about her feelings of inferiority, and even forget where she was.

Following up tenuous clues, building up layer upon layer of information, made her oblivious of everything else and gave her such tremendous satisfaction that she was completely fulfilled. Such absorption in her work compensated Maureen for the fact that, by other people's standards, her private life was drab and monotonous. She had few friends or acquaintances. She spent her evenings and weekends alone . . . reading or working. M&S microwaveable dinners-for-one, and shrink-wrapped sandwiches, were her standby, consumed alone.

She had resigned herself to the fact that she would never marry. Leastways, she had until she met Philip Harmer. Now, for the first time in her life, Maureen allowed herself the luxury of dreaming about what it might be like to share a home with a husband and children.

As the initial research for the project they were working on neared completion, Philip confided in her that it was going to be necessary for him to visit the Far East in order to complete his work. She waited expectantly for him to say he would be needing the services of a researcher. The dilemma of whether or not to accept, if he did invite her to accompany him, became uppermost in her mind.

The idea of the coming separation if he didn't ask her to go with him didn't bear thinking about. It was like waiting for a tempting treat which, deep down, you knew you might not get.

The years were winging by at an alarming rate, and she was well aware that because of her introspective ways she not only lacked friends, and was in something of a rut, but was also missing out on what life could offer.

Normally, Maureen was averse to travelling. Although she was thirty-four she had never even been outside the UK. She considered holidays a waste of time. Lying on a beach didn't appeal to her . . . Not on her *own*! A working trip to the Far East though, with Philip Harmer, would be quite a different proposition.

She switched her thoughts back to the present. Philip was speaking, and she hadn't caught what he'd said . . . Leastways, she didn't think she had. For one moment she thought he'd asked her to marry him!

He gave one of his rare smiles. 'I thought my proposal might take you by surprise, Maureen!'

She remained silent. She felt both exhilaration and disbelief, and was wondering if the wine she had drunk with her meal had turned her daydreams into reality.

'I recognize that, like me, you are career orientated,' Philip Harmer went on. 'That is why I have found working with you both stimulating and rewarding. And why I thought we were so suitable for each other.'

His keen dark eyes studied her shrewdly, watching her reaction with almost clinical detachment. He had always guarded his bachelor existence, partly in the belief that he could only achieve success in his field through undivided dedication, and partly because, as a Roman Catholic, he saw marriage as a lifetime commitment, and, until now, he had never met a woman who had the necessary qualifications to meet his personal standards.

'So, what do you say? Will you marry me?'

She wasn't daydreaming. Philip Harmer really had spoken those magic words. He had asked her to marry him. Maureen felt a surge of excitement; no one had ever proposed to her before. She didn't meet many eligible men. And, normally, the ones she did never gave her a second glance.

Why should they, she reflected disparagingly. She was of medium height, with straight dark hair, dark eyes, and a pursed up mouth that rarely relaxed in a smile. Worst of all, she was painfully thin.

Most of the men she came into contact with during the course of her work were high-powered management with either glamorous partners, or wives and young families, and an established lifestyle.

Professor Philip Harmer wasn't all that young, of course. Early fifties; brain rather than brawn, she thought wryly as she studied his thin frame with its narrow shoulders, his handsome features and greying hair.

Now that she had recovered from her initial shock, the idea of becoming Mrs Philip Harmer had tremendous appeal.

'Well . . .' She studied him discreetly, playing for time because she was not quite sure how to word her acceptance.

His face was inscrutable. Like her, he kept his feelings under control. They could have been discussing statistics for all the emotion he displayed.

'Perhaps you'd like time to think about it . . .?'

'No! No, no. Of course not!' She bit her lip. She didn't want to sound too eager. But neither did she want him to think she wasn't interested.

'Does that mean your answer is yes?'

Maureen nodded.

Leaning across the table he took one of her hands and lifted it to his lips. 'I am most honoured!' he said gravely.

Her tight smile masked her inner surge of contentment. Suddenly, her future had shape; a whole new vista was opening up. As Professor Philip Harmer's wife there would be so much to look forward to; a completely different way of life. Working together they could achieve tremendous success.

'I'm very happy to do so,' she murmured.

'And I'm extremely gratified that you have accepted.' He signalled to the waiter. 'We must drink a toast! Champagne?'

As they clinked glasses he smiled gravely. 'I realize you know very little about me. Or I about you, if it comes to that!'

Maureen smiled politely. She still felt mesmerized.

'Confession time then!' He touched his glass against the side of hers again. 'I'll begin. I'm fifty-three. A bachelor! I'm sound in wind and limb, and a practising Roman Catholic.

You know the sort of work I do so there's nothing more I need tell you about that. You also know that I'm planning an expedition to the Far East quite soon.'

He paused, took a sip of his drink and regarded her solemnly. 'I thought we could have a quiet wedding and make the trip a double event . . . Namely, our honeymoon.'

Maureen took a deep gulp of her champagne and almost choked. Things were moving so swiftly that she felt as if she was being bulldozed along.

'As well as my work, I have private means, and a flat in Portman Mansions,' he went on, mentioning a prestigious block of property outside the town. 'I've never been married and I have no family ties. What else can I tell you?'

Maureen smiled nervously. 'It sounds as though you've led an irreproachable life!'

'I hope so. I've always tried to conform, and to be a law-abiding citizen,' he added a trifle pompously. 'My only brush with authority was when I was twelve. I was caught smoking in the bike shed behind the church by Father Declan, and he threatened to call the police,' he added with an attempt at humour to lighten the tension.

'An exemplary character!'

'Or a dull one. It depends on your outlook,' Philip remarked stiffly. 'Having been brought up Roman Catholic I've always behaved myself because I have a very zealous conscience.'

'It's an admirable quality!' Maureen murmured, her eyes shining. There was a curious old-fashioned dignity about him that she found endearing.

'So now, what about you?'

Maureen shrugged her slim shoulders and looked thoughtful. 'Equally blameless, I think.'

'Go on,' he persisted. 'I want to hear everything right from your schooldays.'

Maureen shrugged. 'OK. After A-levels I spent two years at a business college, and then I went into marketing, specializing in research. Three years ago I started freelancing. For the last six months I've worked exclusively for you.'

'An equally irreproachable life, or so it would seem! Not a single brush with the law? Not even a parking ticket?'

A shadow crossed her face. She avoided his eyes and drained her glass.

He frowned. 'Is there something you've remembered?'

'No . . . no. Nothing . . . nothing at all!'

Her emphatic denial increased his curiosity. 'Look –' he leaned across the table, and took both her hands in his – 'I hold you in very high regard, Maureen. Over the last few months you've become an irreplaceable part of my life. I value you as a friend as well as a colleague. I'm sure neither of us is passionately in love with the other, but for all that, I think marriage between us could work.'

She tried to speak, but failed. She had been aware of the charisma between them right from the moment they had first met. Her feelings for him went far deeper than mere friendship. Even so, she hesitated to tell him how much in love with him she was. He was so reserved that she felt it might embarrass him if she did.

'In my business dealings I have always found complete honesty to be the most manageable way of conducting things. That is why I want us both to know everything there is about each other,' he told her earnestly.

'Yes. Yes, of course! I do understand.'

'I have told you all there is to know about myself. I am simply asking you to do the same.'

'I have!'

He shook his head. 'You've told me very little. I don't even know how old you are!'

Suddenly afraid that Philip Harmer might withdraw his offer of marriage, Maureen became uncharacteristically garrulous.

'I'm thirty-four, and I'm single. I have my own car, and my own home. It's a one-bedroom apartment in a new estate here in Dutton. My parents are still alive, and living in North Wales. They moved there when my father retired. I've already told you all about my career.'

'And you've had no brush with the law . . . Not even when you were a teenager?'

The words were spoken in a jesting tone but she was conscious that he was watching her keenly. She felt a dull flush creep up her neck, gradually suffusing her cheeks.

'No! No! Of course I haven't!' She spread her hands, then covered her face with them, shielding herself from his piercing blue stare.

'There's obviously something you're not telling me,' he persisted in a puzzled voice. 'What is it? If we are going to spend the rest of our lives together I feel I have a right to know,' he added pompously.

'Can I have another glass of champagne!'

He frowned. 'Of course!' He refilled her glass, but didn't join her in a second drink.

The silence between them was an uneasy one.

'Now, what have you to tell me?' He waited expectantly.

Maureen sipped her champagne. 'It was all a long time ago,' she said in a low voice. 'I've never spoken about it to anyone else, except my parents . . .' She hesitated, wishing she'd kept silent, wondering if it was wise to say any more.

'I'm listening.'

'It happened when I was eighteen. The last day at school . . .' She took another drink from her glass.

The champagne sent a surge of euphoria through her, clearing her head, reviving long buried memories.

She felt as if she was being transported back sixteen years. One of an excited crowd of teenagers all clamouring around the notice board in the hall at Benbury Secondary School trying to read their A-level results.

She had been the only girl on the list. The other girls had all been bitterly disappointed. They began teasing her, deriding her achievement, calling her a 'swot'. Boys who had failed, equally jealous of her achievement, had joined in.

The boys whose names were listed alongside hers had insisted she went with them for a celebration drink.

She'd never been in a pub before. They had downed pints of beer or lager, but they'd bought her a whisky and lemonade followed by a gin and tonic. Unused to drink of any kind, she had been legless by the time they left the pub.

The boys were in high spirits. A few blocks up the road five of them had bundled her into a disused shed on the edge of some waste ground. At first they'd been content to force kisses upon her, but it didn't stop at that. As they bantered and teased each other, they'd grown more and more aroused. Egging each other on, the lustful, drink-inflamed teenagers had raped her one after the other, leaving her bruised, battered and almost unconscious.

'Since then, I've avoided men,' she told Philip Harmer in a shaky voice as she finished her account of the incident. She gave a tremulous smile as she looked across at him.

The look of horror on his thin face brought her sharply back to the present as though she'd been doused in cold water.

'Are you telling me you were gang-banged?' he asked incredulously.

'That's rather a crude way of putting it, but in essence I suppose that was what happened,' she admitted hesitantly.

He shuddered. 'I don't believe I'm hearing this!'

She stiffened as she heard the revulsion in his voice. 'It was a long time ago. And it certainly wasn't my fault!' she defended hotly.

Philip Harmer avoided her eyes, but she was acutely aware that he was deeply disturbed by what she had told him.

'Will you excuse me for a moment?' Scraping back his chair he stood up and made for the toilets.

Maureen shook her head like a boxer recovering from a well-aimed punch. She couldn't believe that she had been so stupid. All these years she had never breathed a word to a living soul about what had taken place in that shed on her last day at school. And to blurt it out now! To Philip Harmer of all people! The one person she was most anxious to impress.

The pain deep inside her was like a knife turning in her chest. She felt physically sick. Tears pricked behind her eyelids. She blinked them away, determined not to break down. That would be the final humiliation.

She had almost regained her self-control by the time he returned to the table, but her head was spinning, and she suspected it was because she had drunk too much champagne.

'Could I have a coffee?' she asked muzzily.

There was an uncomfortable silence while they waited for the waiter to bring it.

'When are you planning . . .' Maureen fumbled for the right

words. She didn't think 'for us to get married' were appropriate at the moment so she changed it to: 'To leave on this visit to the Far East?'

Philip Harmer frowned, his mouth pursed. 'I'm not sure. I haven't finalized the exact date of my trip yet.'

'It will be quite soon?'

'Oh yes!' He gave a thin smile. 'No point in delaying matters . . . no point at all.'

She relaxed a little. Now the initial shock had passed it seemed he was taking her revelations in his stride.

Her spirits lifted. That must mean that everything was going to be all right between them, and she had nothing to worry about after all. It had been something of a bombshell for him, but now she'd confessed he would be able to forget all about it, just as she had done all these years.

TWO

Maureen Flynn tried desperately to get to sleep. She tossed and turned, plumped up her pillows, buried her head under the bedclothes, all to no avail. No matter what she did she was unable to blot out from her mind the humiliation and despair she felt following her revelations to Philip Harmer.

She still couldn't believe she had taken such a risk with her own future. She must have been mad! It was like winning the Lottery and then screwing up the ticket instead of collecting the winnings.

Would she ever be able to forget the look of distaste on his thin face when she'd told him that she had once been raped, or was it going to haunt her forever?

To have guarded her shameful secret all these years and then to have blurted it out like she had done was unbelievable! And to Philip Harmer of all people!

What could she have been thinking about? Such utter stupidity! It was bordering on a death wish. He was the first man who had ever penetrated the hard shell she'd built around her feelings. The only man she had ever met who appealed to her as a prospective partner.

The only man who had ever proposed to her!

It wasn't like her to blab about her past. That was a closed book. She'd buried it deep in her subconscious many years ago. Something she'd been determined to forget for ever. Now it was all floating on the surface again.

Her mind seethed with memories as the harrowing experience flooded back into focus. She was back there. In that dank, dirty shed with its cobwebs and dirt floor. She was being jostled by the boys, pushed and pawed, slobbered over.

It had started with wet, beery kisses. First one, then another. Then they were all over her, scrabbling like pigs in a trough. Pushing their wet mouths against her throat and neck.

She'd felt sick and frightened when they'd started pulling at her clothing. Ripping off her school blouse they grabbed at her breasts, squeezing, licking, sucking. When she'd cried out in pain one of them had stuffed a grubby handkerchief in her mouth. She'd kicked and fought, trying to get free, but the more she'd struggled the more frenzied they'd become. They'd behaved like vicious animals

Sandy Franklin had been unspeakably cruel. Tall, raw-boned with a wild shock of red hair, and big, bony hands, he'd been the most callous of them all. He'd been the first one to rape her, goaded into doing so by taunts and jeers from Dennis Jackson.

Jackson had been the oldest of the gang. Head boy. A natural leader. Brainy. Scheming. Sinister, with a vicious streak of cruelty in his make-up.

He'd egged Sandy, and the others, into action. Ordered them to hold her down, to strip off the rest of her clothing. There'd been a gleam of enjoyment in his green eyes when she'd begged him to tell the others to stop.

He could have put an end to them molesting her. They both knew that. One word from him and the others would have held back, but he chose not to. It was obvious from the look on his face that he was experiencing a vicarious thrill from what he was witnessing.

He'd waited until last for his turn.

Maureen felt herself breaking out into a cold sweat as she recalled the unspeakable indignities she'd suffered at his hands. Afterwards, along with the others, he'd taken to his heels. They'd left her lying there in the shed, sobbing.

Bruised and shaken she'd stumbled home. Her parents were shocked and outraged when they heard what had happened, but they told no one, not even the police. So great was their shame that they had refused to even call a doctor!

Trembling and tearful, her mother had bathed her and tended to her cuts and bruises. Then she'd put her to bed with aspirins and hot milk, almost as if nothing untoward had happened.

Next day, when her mother changed the dressings, she refused to discuss the matter. Her father had also ignored the incident, but he had insisted that she should remain indoors until the bruises on her face faded and the swellings subsided. There had been no treatment for the bruising inside her mind.

If she tried to speak about it to her mother, her mother hushed her to silence, telling her it was best if she forgot all about what had happened. She felt too embarrassed even to try and talk to her father about such an incident. He was a formidable man, cynical, with a heart of flint. A dictator in his own home. Her mother not only waited on him hand and foot, but obeyed his every whim. He laid responsibility for what had happened on his wife, blaming her for not warning their daughter against having anything to do with boys.

From then on he had ignored Maureen completely. It was as if by not speaking to her, and pretending she wasn't there, he could forget the entire shameful incident.

A hostile silence invaded their lives. Her mother looked careworn and haggard, her face deathly pale with dark smudges beneath her eyes as though she hadn't slept for weeks.

Maureen remembered how she had cried herself to sleep at night. She'd felt dirty, soiled. Although they had told no one, she felt that everyone she met knew about what had happened.

Looking back, she realized her parents must have felt the same. Later that year they'd moved away from Benbury.

Her mother had been right, though; time was a great healer. She couldn't remember when she had finally stopped crying herself to sleep. It had probably been when she realized that no one else was aware of what had happened, or if they did know, they simply weren't interested.

The move had helped. Once there was no danger of meeting any of the boys who'd been involved in the debacle she'd been able to draw a veil over the experience and, in time, banish it into some deep recess of her mind.

Attending Business School had been the start of an entirely different lifestyle. Nevertheless, she had become very reserved. No one was allowed to penetrate the protective shell she built around her feelings.

Not until now!

It had been a revelation when she first realized that in Philip Harmer she'd at last found a man she could respect and love.

One whose mental talents paralleled her own, and whose aims and ambitions mirrored hers.

Each passing day had brought a sense of astonishment. And tonight had seen the culmination of her most private fantasies. When he had asked her to marry him she had been too overwhelmed for words. It had been difficult not to throw herself into his arms with joy and relief.

Her heart beat wildly as she relived his reaction to her confession. The moment she'd seen the horror on Philip's face she'd wished she'd ignored his plea that she should tell him every detail about her life.

She was sure the only time she'd felt so terrified had been on that harrowing night itself. A chill chased down her back as she remembered what a struggle it had been for him to come to terms with her revelations.

Still unable to sleep, Maureen went to make herself a hot milky drink. By the time she returned to bed she was once more calm, and feeling confident about her future . . . their future together.

She even managed to convince herself she was relieved that she had spoken out. Philip was right; it was better not to have any skeletons in the cupboard. Now, they both knew everything there was to know about each other.

She snuggled down under the covers. It was sheer heaven to have a clear conscience at last, she thought as she drifted off to sleep.

Fingers of light were parting the curtains when she woke. For a moment she lay there wondering why she felt so light-hearted, as if she hadn't a care in the world.

As the events of the previous evening came back to her she smiled contentedly, letting her thoughts linger on the new life that now lay ahead of her.

She wondered how her parents would react when they heard she was to marry Professor Philip Harmer. Would they think he was a trifle old for her? Probably not. At their age they would consider someone in their early fifties merely middle-aged. And they would regard the fact that he was a professor of paramount importance.

Doubtless, too, her mother would find comfort in knowing that at last she was settling down and would not be on her own when they were gone, but would have someone to care for her.

Somebody to care for her!

It would be wonderful to have another person to share her thoughts and experiences. They'd be able to go to the theatre and concerts together. And, of course, they'd travel. The working trip to the Far East, and to Hong Kong for their honeymoon, would be only the first of a great many exciting expeditions.

Humming to herself, she took a shower, her mind still occupied with thoughts of the many changes marriage to Philip Harmer would bring.

She'd be able to give up this place for a start, she thought with a sigh of relief. When she had first moved in to Windermere Mews, having a one bedroom flat all to herself had seemed like heaven. It was only when she began to work as a freelancer that she had realized how cramped it was. In next to no time, bookshelves, computer, printer, and filing cabinets dominated the living room, and even overflowed into the bedroom.

Which was probably why she had become a workaholic, she thought wryly.

She wondered what Philip's flat in Portman Mansions was like. Even though they'd known each other for almost six months, they had never visited each other's homes. Philip would have considered that to be improper.

Flinging back her wardrobe doors she riffled through the clothes hanging there, pushing aside the sombre blacks and greys she usually wore and selecting a pale-blue wool dress that her mother had bought her one Christmas.

From now on, she would pay more attention to what she wore, she resolved as she slipped it on.

She was pleasantly startled by her reflection in the mirror. She looked so different. The dress softened and flattered, making her appear attractively slim. She was suddenly so eager for Philip to see her looking so good that she decided to phone him right away and suggest they meet for coffee. Afterwards they could go shopping for her engagement ring. He hadn't mentioned buying one, and she was sure he hadn't already done so because he was far too practical. He'd wait to make sure she accepted his proposal before taking such a step.

She was pleased in a way. It would have been more romantic if he'd produced it last night, of course, but this way she would be able to choose exactly the sort of ring she wanted, rather than something he thought appropriate!

She held up her left hand, splaying her fingers as if studying a ring on her third finger.

It would have to be fairly unostentatious, though, she mused. He would hate her to wear anything flashy. A solitaire diamond? That would be safest. He'd approve of that.

There was no reply when she dialled his number so she rang off. Often he didn't answer the phone if he was working. She had tried to persuade him to install an answering machine, but he said that would be too distracting. Returning calls would waste valuable time. If people wanted him then they would ring back again.

She pressed the recall button. An instant double ring was the signal that they'd agreed on when she'd first started working for him so that he would know it was her.

She felt puzzled when there was still no reply. She couldn't imagine where he might be so early in the morning. He never left the house before lunchtime. It was one of his strictest maxims.

Perhaps he had gone to buy her a ring!

She went back into the bedroom to collect her coat, bag and car keys. She'd drive round to his flat.

When she reached her front door she stopped to pick up a letter lying on the doormat and felt a thrill of delight when she recognized his writing.

Delivered by hand!

So that was why there had been no answer when she'd phoned. A card, judging by its thickness. And so early in the day! Now that really did show how much he cared, she thought as she tore open the envelope.

It wasn't a card. It was a letter!

As she unfolded the single sheet of thick notepaper

something fluttered to the ground. When she picked it up, she was mystified to find it was a cheque. A cheque for £5,000!

Colour rushed to her cheeks. Surely Philip didn't expect her to go shopping for an engagement ring on her own?

As she read the brief note that accompanied the cheque the colour drained from Maureen's face. Her throat felt so constricted that she could barely breathe, and there was a violent pounding in her temples.

Tight-jawed, trembling with humiliation, she read the note again. The words 'fee for the work you've undertaken', 'special bonus', and 'termination of our contract' branded themselves on to her mind.

Her eyes blurred with tears, and that made her angrier still. As she brushed them away her rage turned to hatred.

Hatred for Philip Harmer.

She'd never forgive him for this. He had opened the door to a future that offered the culmination of her private dreams and fantasies, only to slam it in her face!

To reject her love, to spurn her, after she'd accepted his proposal of marriage, was unbelievable!

And all because she had done as he had asked her to do and bared her soul to him. By confessing that she had once been raped, she had forfeited his respect.

She shuddered. Why had she been so honest? She should have said nothing. It had taken such a tremendous effort to come to terms with what had happened that she should have left the memory buried deep in her subconscious, as it had been all these years.

Seething with rage and frustration she picked up the phone again. This time she let it ring. She wouldn't use their special code. She didn't want him to know it was her.

There was still no reply, and slowly it dawned on her that there never would be.

He had no further use for her. He had tossed her aside like a broken doll. In his eyes she was soiled, tainted, defiled.

She picked up the cheque, prepared to tear it into a thousand tiny pieces. Her pay off! Wages for services rendered! She laughed hysterically. And she'd thought it was to buy an engagement ring!

There was no engagement! There would be no wedding! There would be no further contact. His brief note made that very plain.

Stunned and furious, she quivered with mindless rage. She hated Philip Harmer with a savage vehemence.

But that was insignificant compared with the overpowering malevolence she felt towards the boys who'd ruined her life all those long years ago.

THREE

Benbury sparkled in the sharp March sunshine. Flowering cherry trees and early daffodils set the bright stamp of spring on the town. In spite of the keen wind it was a glorious day.

The house in Mayling Street where Maureen had been born, and had grown up, looked smaller than she remembered. It had a dejected air. The net curtains at the upstairs windows needed a wash, and the silk flowers in the downstairs front-room window looked as though they'd been thrust into the black and white vase more as a means of getting rid of them than with any real thought.

White paint was flaking off the bedroom window sills, and the black front door was chipped and scratched. It had never looked like that when she'd lived there. Her mother had been most fastidious, and, regular as clockwork, her father had given the outside of the house a coat of paint every springtime.

Her mother had changed the curtains twice a year. She had hung up crisp floral cotton ones in April and changed them for heavy velvet drapes in October to keep out any winter draughts.

Maureen's own bedroom had been at the back of the house. There had been a huge horse-chestnut tree right outside the window, dominating the long, narrow strip of garden.

She'd loved that tree; had considered it her friend and carved her name on its bark. In late spring it had been covered with clusters of erect white flowers, like candles. In autumn it had provided a rich harvest of glossy conkers that everyone at school had wanted, especially the boys, so she'd filled her pockets with them for the sheer thrill of handing them out. Her face hardened. Dennis Jackson and John Moorhouse had been two of those boys. In those days she'd thought of them as her friends.

She let out the clutch and moved away. That had been a long

time ago! She drove on, turning right, turning left, and then right again. The school was still there. She pulled in and surveyed the red-brick building with its tall narrow windows. A new wing had been added. It was like a huge concrete finger jutting out at one side, swallowing up part of the playing field.

She gripped the wheel. It was sixteen years since she'd lived in Benbury, since that horrendous day that had changed her life. She didn't want to dwell on it . . . not yet.

Tight-lipped, she drove on.

As she circled the town she found there were a great many changes. The new housing estates of pseudo-Elizabethan boxes, new factories and office blocks had almost doubled the size of Benbury. It was now a thriving modern town with countless mini-roundabouts, several new petrol stations, and an enormous glass and chrome car-showroom.

She drove slowly down the High Street looking for somewhere to park, surprised to find double yellow lines edging the pavement on both sides from one end to the other.

She recalled there had been a parking area adjacent to the library so she made her way there, found a space for her red Ford Escort, and parked up.

It was only a few minutes' walk back to the High Street through the park. That was where she had pushed her doll's pram when she was very small, and where she'd ridden her two wheel bicycle for the first time.

The pond, where she had been taken every Sunday by her father to feed the ducks, had been filled in and was now a formal flower bed, bright with daffodils and primroses. One corner of the park had been turned into a playground with swings and a climbing frame.

The High Street was much busier than she remembered it. There were now two supermarkets, two chemist's, a health food shop, three greengrocer's, two carpet shops, a toy shop, four hairdresser's, a furniture store, a large newsagent's, a hardware shop, several boutiques, half a dozen estate agents, and several cafes and restaurants, as well as two pubs and a wine bar.

She walked up one side of the road, and then back down the other. Side roads that had once been residential were now crammed with small specialist shops. There was a beauty salon, a home-furnishing emporium, a jeweller's, an Oxfam shop, and a betting shop in one of them. In another, a dentist, a shoe repairer's, and two more charity shops.

There were quite a few people about, muffled up against the bright cold. She looked searchingly at each of them, wondering if she would see anyone she recognized.

The passing years would have changed most of them, she mused. Girls she'd been at school with would now be in their mid-thirties and either established in a career, the same as she was, or married with young children. People of her parents' generation would be elderly, grey-haired . . . changed out of all recognition.

She went into one of the cafes for a coffee, carrying her tray across to a table by the window so that she could study the passers-by as she waited for the coffee to cool.

Most of the women about her own age were pushing prams or holding toddlers by the hand. Unfamiliar faces shopping for food for their families. She wondered how many of them had lived in the town all their lives. Probably not many! Most of them would have been drawn to Benbury by the new estates and factories that had mushroomed on the periphery of the town.

It made her feel like an interloper; as if she had no right to be there.

Why was she doing this, punishing herself in this way, she asked herself. What was to be gained from coming back to Benbury? The town had nothing but bad memories for her. Why torment herself like this? It was like picking a scab, or rubbing salt into an open wound.

It would be far more sensible to forget the humiliation that had forced her and her parents to leave Benbury. Bury it deep in her subconscious the same as she had done before.

It had remained dormant all these years so why resurrect it!

What was the old adage her father was so fond of repeating? *Let sleeping dogs lie.*

She should have known that Philip Harmer's proposal would come to nothing. The very fact that she had fallen in love with him was enough to put a jinx on their relationship, she thought bitterly. Rejection was part of her destiny!

Even her own parents had rejected her after the rape. They'd tried to hide it, of course, but things had never been the same between the three of them. There had been a strange, nervous atmosphere, even after they'd moved away from Benbury.

They'd made a superficial protest when she'd said she was leaving home, but they'd made no real attempt to stop her. They'd even given her the deposit to buy a flat in Dutton.

If only Philip Harmer hadn't asked her to marry him, she could have borne it. She had actually reconciled herself to the fact that her work stint for him had come to an end. Hoping he might ask her to go with him on his Far East trip had simply been a pipe-dream, a harmless diversion to soften the parting.

As she sipped her coffee, and stared out of the window, she noticed the name 'Franklin and Son' on the newsagent's directly across the street from the cafe.

Her cup rattled against the saucer as she put it down.

Sandy Franklin had been one of the boys involved, and his father had owned a newsagent's shop.

The hairs on the back of her neck prickled. To be so close to one of the boys who'd been involved sent shudders through her. She wondered if any of the others were still living in Benbury.

Maureen steeled herself to go into the newsagent's when she left the cafe, convincing herself that it would lay one ghost to rest, at least. At the last moment her nerve deserted her, and she backed off. She wasn't ready to come face to face with Sandy Franklin . . . Not yet.

It must have been Fate that had made her decide to park by the library, she told herself as she hurried back to where she'd left her car. This was a research job she was going to enjoy.

Her briefcase was in the car boot. She took out a clipboard and pen. Once in the library she headed straight for the reference section. Twenty minutes later, she had all the information she wanted: the addresses and telephone numbers of the boys who'd raped her.

There was one more thing she needed . . . A street map.

Her mind busy with details, she walked back to the High Street. The newsagent's would be the only shop likely to stock a comprehensive street map. Buoyed up with the success of her research, this time she had no qualms about going in.

The shop was busy, so Maureen browsed through the various racks of magazines and paperbacks looking for what she wanted. There were no maps at all, not even in the miscellaneous section.

'Can I help you?'

She'd been so engrossed that she hadn't noticed a tall rangy man dressed in slacks and a sweater approach her.

She looked up and did a double take. Her pulse hammered. She couldn't be mistaken. It *was* Sandy Franklin. She would have known him anywhere. He was older, of course, but otherwise he hadn't altered a great deal. His wild shock of red hair had been tamed by a short back and sides, but his raw-boned face and hooded grey eyes were an indelible part of her memory of that terrible day.

She bit her lip, swallowing back the bile that rose in her throat at the recollection, conscious that he was waiting for her to answer.

'I'm looking for a street map . . . Do you stock them?'

'I think I can find you one.'

He walked towards the counter and began sorting through the contents of a rotary metal stand that stood near the till.

As she watched his bony hands at work she found that it took every vestige of will power not to cry out, not to run out into the street. She could feel them on her body, kneading her flesh, poking, probing. A shudder went through her. She wanted to get as far away from him as possible.

'Here you are, have a look through these.' He spread out a selection of local maps for her inspection.

He obviously hadn't recognized her . . . not yet, at any rate, she thought with relief as she selected the map she decided would be most useful.

There was still no glimmer of recognition on Sandy Franklin's face as she paid him. He popped her purchase inside a bag printed with the shop's name, address and phone number, and handed it to her.

Maureen found it hard to believe that he'd failed to remember her. She had known it was him the minute he'd spoken, even before she'd seen his red hair and prominent features.

It was better this way, of course. She felt exultant; it left her more in control of the situation.

She returned to her car and spread out the map on the roof. Referring to the list she'd drawn up in the library, Maureen pinpointed where the other four lived.

The High Street had been the only listing for the name Franklin, so she assumed that Sandy lived over the shop. Not that it mattered. She knew now where she could locate him.

She wrote down the names of John Moorhouse, Dennis Jackson and Brian Patterson in the margin of the map, and gave each of them an identifying number. Next she located the road in which each of them lived and circled it in red. There wasn't enough room to write in each name so she added the appropriate reference number.

It was now almost midday. Stowing the clipboard into the boot of her car she slipped a notebook into her handbag along with the map. Then she locked up the car and went to find somewhere to have lunch.

There were plenty of places to choose from in the High Street, but in the end Maureen decided it would be either the Eatery or the Benbury Arms. She studied the menu on the window of the Eatery, an upmarket restaurant, and decided she didn't really want a three-course meal, so she settled for the pub.

It was not quite half past twelve, so there were not a great many customers in the Benbury Arms. The two men who were leaning on the lounge bar counter chatting earnestly to each other moved to one side to make way for her.

'A glass of dry white wine, please,' she told the fresh-faced young barman.

'And something to eat?' He passed her a printed menu card. She ordered a cheese omelette and a side salad.

He wrote out her bill and passed her the top copy. 'Take a seat, and we'll bring it over to you when it's ready. We call out the number on your bill,' he added.

Maureen thanked him and made her way to a window seat. She angled her chair so that she could keep an eye on everyone who came into the pub as well as those who walked by in the street outside. So far she hadn't seen a single soul she recognized except Sandy Franklin. Yet she had known countless people when she'd lived in Benbury.

While she waited for her omelette she studied the map, particularly the roads she'd circled in red. They were well scattered. It could be an interesting afternoon locating them all, she mused as she sipped her wine.

She wondered how they would react if she knocked on the door and reminded them of who she was.

'Here you are then,' a cheery voice said, bringing Maureen out of her reverie.

'I'm sorry! I didn't hear you call out the number,' she apologized. She scrabbled the map out of the way so that the plump, smiling woman, wearing a pink overall over her black skirt and white blouse, could set down the plate of food she was holding.

The woman laughed. 'That's because I didn't bother to shout it out. Not many in yet so I knew it must be for you.' She handed Maureen cutlery wrapped in a pink serviette. 'We don't get busy until one o'clock. Then it's all go for a while. All the business people come in then, you see.'

'Yes. Yes, of course.' Maureen folded up the map. 'This looks very nice.'

'Hope you enjoy it.'

Maureen tucked in. For a few minutes she forgot the purpose of her visit, forgot the plan that had been forming in her mind ever since she'd walked into the newsagent's and recognized Sandy Franklin.

She was halfway through her meal when the barmaid came back to ask if everything was alright.

'Yes, fine! The omelette is delicious.'

She watched the woman go back to the bar. She was about thirty-five, and Maureen wondered if they'd been at school together. Rather funny if we were and neither of us remembers the other, she thought wryly.

She was still thinking about it when Sandy Franklin walked in. She felt a moment's panic in case he recognized her as one of his customers earlier in the day.

So what if he does! He doesn't know who I am or he would have mentioned it in the shop, she reminded herself.

Rubbing his bony hands together, he strode up to the bar, a huge grin on his freckled face. The woman who had brought her food was standing on the pub side of the bar, and Sandy grabbed her round the waist, making her squeal.

'Pint of the best, Fred,' he ordered the owner, his arm still encircling the woman's waist.

'Well, let's have Peggy back this side of the bar, and then she'll pull it for you.'

'She can do that without going behind the bar,' Sandy guffawed. His hand slid down over the woman's buttocks before she could move away.

Maureen's mouth tightened. Sandy Franklin hadn't changed. Not one iota. She shuddered as his laugh rang out, coarse, obscene. She sensed the embarrassment the woman was feeling, and anger against Sandy Franklin flamed up inside her. It was almost as if once again she was being pushed down on to the floor in the filthy hut, and in the background was that awful braying guffaw.

She pushed aside the unfinished omelette, her appetite gone. She took a gulp of wine, but it tasted as sour as the bile that had risen in her throat. She needed a coffee.

She was trembling so much that she was afraid to stand up to go and order one. Anyway, there was only one counter in the lounge bar, and Sandy Franklin was still dominating it.

The realization that she'd have to walk past the bar to get out of the pub filled her with dread. It would mean walking so close to Sandy Franklin that she could touch him. Or he could touch her!

The feeling of being soiled and dirty, which she'd experienced when she'd been raped, came flooding back. Her palms felt moist, and there were beads of perspiration dampening her brow.

She felt vengeful, filled with a raw impulse to lash out at Sandy Franklin: to inflict some terrible, irrevocable damage, an injury that would remain with him for the rest of his life.

Not just Sandy Franklin, either! She wanted the others to

suffer too. Mentally as well as physically; the same as she had done all these years.

Her day was ruined. Now, all she wanted to do was to go home to Dutton. Bolt the door of her flat in Windermere Mews. Barricade herself in.

All her plans had turned sour. She wasn't going to lay any ghosts by coming to Benbury, she thought ruefully; she'd only resurrected them!

FOUR

John Moorhouse turned into the driveway of Twenty-Seven Fieldway, and carefully negotiated his Rover into the garage, skimming past the two small mountain bikes that had been abandoned just inside the doors.

How many times have I told Malcolm and Danny to park up tight against the wall, he thought irritably as he killed the engine. He'd give them one final warning. They had to learn to do as they were told.

It was easier to control a mixed class of thirty fourteen-year-old boys than it was those two, he thought wryly as he struggled to open his car door back far enough for him to get out without dropping the pile of exercise books that he'd brought home to mark.

The stillness of an empty house greeted him as he let himself in. It was Thursday. Marilyn and the boys were at Cubs.

After a day in the classroom, bombarded by the deafening noises that seemed to make up school life, the utter silence was sheer bliss.

Dumping his briefcase and the pile of books he was carrying on to the hall table, he went into the lounge and across to the drinks cabinet to pour himself a whisky.

He didn't normally take a drink until late in the evening. A whisky for him and brandy for Marilyn. It was their special treat, a little reward to help them unwind once Malcolm and Danny, their eight-year-old twins, were safely tucked up in bed.

After a leisurely supper, which they ate from trays on their lap unless they had invited friends over, they would spend the rest of the evening reading, watching television or listening to music.

Though that also depended on how much homework marking there was to be done. If there was a lot then Marilyn would help by checking spellings and grammar, leaving him to deal with the text relating to the subjects he specialized in: History, Geography and English.

Tonight, although he had brought an armful of year eleven books home, he wouldn't work on them until much later, and then only if there was nothing on the TV worth watching.

Thursday was his night to put his feet up and relax, at least until eight o' clock when Marilyn and the two boys came home from Cubs.

He'd laughed when she'd first told him that she was going to become Cub Mistress.

'What the hell for? Don't you see enough of the boys as it is? I would have thought you'd be glad to get them out of your hair for an hour or two.'

She'd shrugged her slim shoulders and pushed her curtain of blonde hair back from her round face, her blue eyes dancing. 'I've fallen for the Scout Master,' she told him in an exaggerated whisper.

They'd both curled up at her joke. Henry Wood was at least fifty, and with his military bearing, pencil moustache, and clipped manner, he was more like a pocket-size Hitler than a heart-throb.

'Seriously, why have you decided to become involved?'

'The boys have to be there at half six, it's a twenty minute drive, and they finish at eight. What's the point of driving home, and then having to go back for them in an hour's time?'

He shrugged. 'You've always left them in the past.'

'True! It was all right when the Simpsons lived five minutes away, and I could pop in and have a coffee with Mary. Since they moved I either have to wait in the car, or sit at one end of the hall and read a book, so I decided that as I'm there I may as well help out.'

'If that's what you want to do, darling. Otherwise you take them, and I'll collect them.'

Marilyn had opted to stay and lend a hand with the Cubs.

At first John had resented coming home to an empty house. He'd found himself wandering around aimlessly, going from one room to the next, wondering what to do. He kept looking at his watch, unable to bring himself to tackle any of the jobs that needed his attention because he knew Marilyn and the boys would be home in half an hour or so.

But once he'd settled into the routine, he found himself looking forward to his evening alone. He even made sure he finished promptly, planning his timetable so that he was never responsible for supervising games or any other extra-curriculum activities on a Thursday.

Two hours of doing whatever he wanted to do without anyone interrupting him, without the boys demanding he should play games with them, or Marilyn wanting him to change a light bulb, or fix a dripping tap. Two hours of utter relaxation.

It was sheer bliss!

He switched on the television, then walked across to the walnut-fronted drinks cabinet, selected a cut glass tumbler and picking up a bottle of Scotch unscrewed the bottle with pleasurable anticipation.

His back was to the door, his attention focused on the deep lilting voice of Huw Edwards reading the news, so he didn't hear the footsteps crossing the hall. Nor was he aware that the sitting room door had opened, and that someone had come into the room.

The slim figure, anonymous in a black cagoule, the hood screening the face almost completely from view, moved swiftly across the room to where John Moorhouse stood pouring his drink.

Without uttering a word, the figure raised an arm above John Moorhouse's back. There was a momentary glint of steel. The bottle in John Moorhouse's hand crashed down on to the tumbler, shattering it.

Fumes of spilled whisky filled the air as, with a groan, John Moorhouse slid to the floor.

The figure hovered like a black vulture over its fallen prey. Then, placing one foot on John Moorhouse's back, the attacker grasped hold of the weapon with both hands, and withdrew it, wiping the bloodied metal tip backwards and forwards down the victim's trouser leg to clean it.

The dark-clad figure turned the body over, prodding at it, then listening with obvious satisfaction to the agonized gasps that signalled that John Moorhouse was still conscious.

The last thing John Moorhouse was aware of before he lost consciousness was the ultimate humiliation of knowing that his dark-grey trousers had been unzipped, his pale-blue cotton shirt and his striped boxer shorts ripped open so that he was semi-nude.

The dark-cloaked intruder carefully studied the result with a satisfied smile.

It was the supreme revenge.

There was nothing left to do. It was time to leave.

'John . . . John. We're home!' Marilyn Moorhouse called out as she unlocked the front door and pushed it open. 'What on earth are you doing sitting in the dark? Have you got a migraine or something?' she called out as she switched on the hall light.

There was no reply.

Danny and Malcolm rushed past her. 'Mum! Can we watch telly while we have our supper?' they begged as they shed their anoraks and scarves, dropping them in the hallway.

'No, you most certainly can't! Pick up your coats, and hang them up properly,' she ordered, 'or it's up to bed with no supper.'

With cheeky grumbling they did as they were told.

'Right, that's better. Now, into the kitchen for a snack, and then straight up to bed.'

'Can we just watch while you get our supper ready . . . please,' they begged in chorus.

'No. No, no, no!' she told them emphatically, grabbing at Malcolm as he made a dash for the sitting room door.

'But, Mum . . .'

'Into the kitchen for a snack, or straight upstairs to bed,' she said firmly.

The next half hour was a battle of wills.

Marilyn finally won. She tucked them both into bed, kissed them goodnight, and shut the bedroom door firmly on their overtired, whingeing voices.

Cubs was all very well, she thought as she made her way downstairs, but late nights just didn't seem to agree with her two. Once they were past their usual bedtime they seemed to take on a new lease of life, albeit a grouchy one.

There was still no light showing under the sitting room door so Marilyn went straight back into the kitchen. She'd waken John with a coffee.

First, she rinsed the cups the boys had used, and tidied around. Then she loaded their coffee, and the biscuit tin, on a tray. Balancing it on one hand she pushed open the sitting room door, and switched on the light.

'Wakey-wakey! I know you're in there skulking in the dark, pretending to be asleep so that you don't have to help get the two little horrors off to bed,' she said breezily.

For a split second she stood transfixed, her eyes wide with disbelief at the sight of John sprawled in front of the drinks cabinet. Her breath caught in her throat. Her mind refused to take in the details.

The loaded tray she was carrying tilted forward but she was powerless to do anything to save it. Even when it crashed to the ground, splattering her feet with scalding liquid as the coffee cascaded, she remained motionless in the doorway. Her heart was pounding. Her jaw sagged. A scream froze in her throat.

What could have happened? How could he have collapsed in such an ungainly sprawl? A heart attack? Not at his age! And his clothes? Why were they in such disarray that he was lying there fully exposed?

She shuddered convulsively as the details of the spectacle in front of her registered. Her hand flew to her mouth. Her own strident breathing unnerved her. She knew she was on the point of hysteria.

Was he really dead? She needed help. She chewed down on her bottom lip, unsure of what to do. She gulped in air, knowing she must on no account cry out because, if she did, she would rouse the two boys.

She shivered uncontrollably. Thank God she had insisted on them going straight to bed! Supposing she had said they could watch telly and they'd come into the sitting room on their own! She covered her eyes with her hands. It didn't bear thinking about.

The spasm of shivering magnified, taking hold of her entire body, paralysing her with cold, sick fear.

She wrapped her arms round herself to try and control the shaking. She had never felt so terrified in her life.

Who had done such a thing?

And why?

It was so obscene! She had never witnessed anything so monstrous in her life.

And what did she do now? He must be dead. He wouldn't lie there in that condition if he was still alive!

She couldn't leave him lying there.

Nor could she bring herself to touch him. She was no prude, but even though they'd been married for almost ten years they'd always maintained a marked degree of respect for each other's privacy.

It was one of the things she found so endearing about John. He was so sensitive about her feelings, and always behaved with the utmost decorum. In fact, obsessively so!

When they'd first started going out together she'd been amused at how reticent he was about petting.

She had become so worried about his diffidence towards her that she'd even asked her best friend, Sandra Williams, if she thought there was anything odd about him.

'What do you mean by odd?' Sandra's eyes had widened. 'You don't mean you think he's . . . well, you know!'

'I'm not sure. He seems so . . . so sort of backwards-in coming-forwards when we're on our own.'

Sandra had giggled. 'Perhaps it's you . . . Perhaps you turn him off!'

'In that case then, why does he ask me out?'

Sandra had shrugged. 'Perhaps he likes being seen with you because you're so petite. You make him feel big, and strong, and macho.'

'He is big and strong. I'm quite sure he doesn't need me to make him feel macho.'

'Well, you're still the exact opposite to him in looks. You've got long blonde hair, blue eyes, and a round baby face. He's got short dark hair, dark eyes, and a severe, square face . . .'

Marilyn had felt cheated. 'Forget it,' she'd told Sandra. 'You haven't a clue.'

'That's right, I haven't. I've always thought that being opposites you were well suited, if you know what I mean.'

Marilyn had sighed, her blue eyes dreamy. 'I am crazy about him!' she admitted. 'I only wish he was a bit more passionate.'

When John had asked her to marry him, Marilyn could stand the uncertainty no longer. It took a lot of courage to summon up the nerve to talk to him about what she'd come to believe was shyness on his part, but she was determined to do so. She'd been on the pill for over three months in anticipation of them making love, and she felt it was important to clear the air, and discuss the situation.

John had been both embarrassed and evasive, but she had insisted on an answer.

'I thought you'd prefer not to rush things. I thought you'd want to wait until we were married before . . . before . . . you know what I mean.'

On their wedding night they'd both been nervous, but he had been far more apprehensive than her.

'I'm sorry, but I'm afraid of hurting you, Marilyn,' he whispered apologetically as he held her close.

I'll scream if you do,' she teased, hoping to put him at ease.

It had the opposite effect. His face had gone chalk-white, and his eyes had darkened with fear. 'No! Please don't scream, my darling. Whatever you do, don't scream. I couldn't bear it if that happened.'

It had taken months to reassure him, and even longer to reach even a degree of satisfaction for either of them.

All his fears had surfaced again when she'd been expecting the twins. He'd barely touched her after she told him she was pregnant. His excuse was always the same; he was afraid he might hurt her. Even his kisses were chaste, as if she was as brittle as glass.

He'd refused point blank to stay with her when she went into labour.

'I couldn't bear to be there, and see you in so much pain and distress,' he told her. 'Please don't make me! I'll stay at the hospital. I'll come and see you the moment it's all over.'

After the twins were born, John's apparent lack of sex-drive hadn't seemed to matter. Malcolm and Danny had taken up so much of her time that love-making had taken second place anyway. She'd even been glad that he wasn't very demanding.

So why was he lying there in that state with his clothing in such an incredibly revealing state of disarray?

The fears she'd harboured about his sexuality surfaced anew, and even though she struggled to push them aside she couldn't help wondering if he did enjoy a vicarious sex life that she knew nothing about. Had he been entertaining another man when something untoward, like a heart attack, had happened?

If only she could switch off the light, go out of the room, and then come back in again and find John snoozing in his armchair asleep, just as she had expected to do.

If only this was a delusion, or a practical joke, and everything was perfectly normal.

Scalding hot tears slowly oozed between her lids and trickled down her cheeks. Anguished tears. She felt a sense of bewilderment. Confusion. She didn't know what to do for the best. And John couldn't help her.

He would have known what to do! He always did.

Calmly, logically, no matter what the problem was, John always coped. This time, when she most needed him, he couldn't help!

Hesitantly, Marilyn walked towards her husband, and then crouched down beside him. His dark eyes stared unseeingly. Nervously, she placed a hand on his neck, just below his left ear, to check if there was a pulse. She could feel nothing. There was no rise and fall of his chest. She held her fingers over his gaping mouth to verify if he really had stopped breathing. She could feel nothing. She felt for the pulse at his wrist. Again, nothing.

She tried to gather her wits. Was it too late to try resuscitation? She wasn't even too sure how to go about it. They'd done it at Cubs, but that was before she had started to play an active part there, and she had only a hazy recollection of what was involved.

Perhaps if she rolled him on to his side, in the recovery position, it might help. She could remember the diagrams about that. Grabbing hold of his shoulders she began to move him.

It was then that she saw the blood. It was underneath his body in a dark-red mass that began seeping out over the carpet. Rank, red, glutinous. Bile rose into the back of her throat, and her stomach lurched as she gagged noisily.

For a moment she seethed with anger. Not against whoever had done this shocking thing, but against John for not being able to sort things out for her.

She needed to hear his calm, placating voice, listen to him rationalizing about what procedures must be taken, providing a satisfactory explanation.

Why had this terrible thing happened? To him of all people!

Slowly, the pounding in her temples began to subside only to be replaced by the chilling realization that the murderer could still be in the house.

She knew she must get help, but who should she call? The police?

Why hadn't she thought of that, she wondered guiltily. She should have phoned them the moment she'd opened the sitting room door and found John lying there in that state.

She looked round for something to cover him over with, then hid her face with her hands and gave an anguished moan. She couldn't do it.

The police wouldn't want her to touch him, she reminded herself. It was important to leave him exactly as she'd found him. Even covering him over might destroy valuable evidence.

She shuddered at the thought of what lay ahead once the police were notified. All the questions, the probing into their private lives, curiosity from friends and neighbours, and the shame when it was all reported in the newspapers.

Why, oh why had such a terrible thing happened . . . to John of all people!

FIVE

There seemed to be speed cameras everywhere, even on the stretches of the dual carriageway between Benbury and Dutton.

Maureen Flynn clenched the steering wheel so tightly that her neck and shoulders ached. Her urge to travel in excess of the regulation speed was so great that the calf muscles of her right leg were knotted with the strain of controlling the accelerator pedal so that she kept within the law.

She had made the fifty-mile journey so many times in the last ten days that she knew not only every twist and bend in the road, but every bump as well.

She breathed a sigh of relief as her headlights picked out factories and office buildings that marked the start of the industrial estate, and then a black and white road sign proclaiming she'd reached the outskirts of Dutton.

In ten more minutes she would be home. It would take another ten to unload the car, and after that she would be able to relax in a hot bath and soak away the stress of the past few hours. After that she would have a good stiff drink to celebrate.

She smiled to herself. That was nonsense, and she knew it. She didn't feel in the least bit stressed. She felt exhilarated. She always did when she'd completed an undertaking to her complete satisfaction. She prided herself on her competency, on her thoroughness and attention to every aspect.

Every detail had to be right. One missing bit of the jigsaw and she felt on edge. She would spend days researching or checking one seemingly trivial point in order to make sure that even the minutest detail was absolutely correct. Her work was always flawless, faultless and infallible.

She was a perfectionist. That was why she had decided to go freelance. The marketing company where she'd worked, after she'd qualified in Business Studies, had grown too large and far too commercialized. They seemed more concerned in providing the results the client hoped to receive rather than ensuring the information they gave them was in-depth and completely accurate.

When the client was impressed, Maureen found that her superior, Mark Carling, accepted the accolade; when there were brickbats, she was the one expected to field them.

'I am quite prepared to accept responsibility when it's the result of an error on my part, but I'm not going to be used as a scapegoat,' she told him angrily.

'We work as a team so—'

Maureen had seen red. 'Then as the team leader you should be the one to accept all responsibility; the criticism as well as the praise,' she'd interrupted.

It had been like declaring war. The other members of the staff sided with Mark. They were not directly involved. They simply keyed into a computer whatever information was handed to them. They didn't have to meet any clients. In Maureen's estimation they were human robots in every way.

'I couldn't believe my ears when you flared up at Mark like that,' Cindy Little, Mark's secretary, commented when they met in the Ladies cloakroom later that day. 'You're usually so quiet!'

Maureen shrugged. 'I don't see why I should take the blame for his inefficiency,' she said abruptly.

As Cindy carefully renewed her lipstick their eyes met in the mirror. 'You're the one who does the research,' she said pointedly.

'I work from his brief! If Mark doesn't understand what the client wants then he should let me talk to them.'

Cindy shrugged her slim shoulders non-committally but her grey eyes narrowed, and Maureen knew she had said more than she should have done.

Next day, Mark Carling had called her into his office. He didn't ask her to sit down, but kept her standing in front of his desk like an errant junior. Tilting back in his black leather swing chair he stared at her insolently. His small mouth was pursed, as if he was savouring the words he was about to utter like some juicy morsel.

Maureen guessed that Cindy had reported their conversation.

'I understand you don't approve of my methods. You seem to think you should be the one to meet clients, and be briefed by them direct?'

She said nothing, refusing to be goaded into an argument. Confrontations weren't her style. She watched his plump face darken, his foxy opaque eyes fill with hate.

'I suppose you think you could do my job better than I can?'

Again she refused to be drawn. There was no point in starting a battle she couldn't win. She'd done her research and knew he was the company chairman's brother-in-law.

Six weeks later she'd left the marketing company where she'd worked for almost ten years, and then she'd set up on her own as a freelance researcher.

She thought back over some of the more intricate research projects she handled since she'd been working solo, comparing her reaction when each of them had ended with her present mood.

She'd always felt a tremendous sense of satisfaction whenever a client complimented her on her efficiency. This time she had the dual role of being both the client and the operator, and she felt more than mere satisfaction – she felt tremendous gratification.

The days and nights of careful planning had paid off, as she had intended it should do. Meticulous attention to detail was the key to successful research. Now it was proving to be equally effective when applied to materialistic matters, she thought smugly.

The moment she'd read Philip Harmer's letter, and realized why he'd withdrawn his proposal of marriage, she'd resolved to be revenged. And not just against him, but also against those who had been initially responsible.

She had used the same methods as if she had been working for a client. It was the only way to keep her emotions under control.

Until she'd met Philip Harmer she had always kept her relationship with her clients on a strictly business basis.

He had been the one exception. And look where that had landed her, she thought resentfully. By letting her emotions intrude she'd become vulnerable. By allowing herself to fall in love with him she'd suffered heartbreak and humiliation. And she'd also lost a valuable client.

Even worse, by making a pilgrimage to Benbury she'd resurrected ghosts from her past!

This time, though, she intended to lay every one of those ghosts. Permanently! They'd never trouble her again, she was determined to make quite sure of that.

The tension she'd felt while driving eased once she was home. After garaging her Escort she carried the black leather grip, which held the equipment she'd taken with her to Benbury, indoors.

That would be her first job, Maureen decided. Checking to make sure she hadn't left anything behind, and then sorting and storing away anything she would need for future use and, of course, disposing of the rest.

She'd always prided herself on her efficient filing methods. It was an essential part of her stock in trade to allocate a new file to each new undertaking and give it an identifying code name and number.

Then she collated and subdivided the information she collected until she had built up a complete background picture. Only then did she enter all the details into her computer where she would sift and sort, check and double-check, set up comparison tables and pie-charts before printing out a comprehensive dossier.

Each undertaking required different methods as well as patience, thoroughness, and painstaking attention to detail and logic. In some ways it was like puzzling out a complex jigsaw. Months of hard concentrated research could amount to nothing because of a single elusive piece.

In the same way, of course, an obscure fact could be the key that spelled success. A seemingly fruitless task could suddenly gel; it could be the crowning touch and signal another satisfied client.

Mostly, because she worked at home, her clients had no idea of the gruelling struggles needed to unravel the problem they set her. She preferred it that way. She had her own methods and disliked having to listen to other people's opinions or concede to their methods.

Philip Harmer had been the exception. His mind was as analytical as her own, and he was able to think laterally, the same as she often did. His responses had been like an extension of her own mind.

It was too late now, of course, but she bitterly regretted not keeping her own counsel even with him. What on earth had induced her to let down her reserve after so many years of silence?

If only she had stopped to think instead of letting her heart rule her head. How could she have forgotten her mother's anguish about what people would think if they ever found out that she had been raped?

Her mother had even refused to let her see a doctor because she had been afraid he might report what had happened to the police. She couldn't face the public shame.

Her father had been as adamant as her mother. 'Think what it would mean if this got out!' he railed. 'Who would believe your story once people knew you'd gone to a public house drinking with a bunch of boys!'

She tried to defend herself. 'You don't understand,' she protested. 'We were all so excited at passing. Only six of us out of a class of thirty!'

'Six?'

'That's right. Me and five boys.'

'You told us there were four . . . that four boys raped you.'

'One of the boys was sick when we came out of the pub . . . The others left him behind.'

'He shouldn't have been in the pub drinking in the first place . . . none of you should.'

'We wanted to do something crazy . . . to celebrate . . .'

'You did that all right!' her father interrupted bitterly.

They'd talked and argued that night until her brain was in a spin, trying to decide the best way to hush matters up.

Her feelings had been ignored completely, she thought resentfully. The important factor in her parent's eyes was that the school year had ended. She wouldn't be going back to school, so she need never see anything of the boys who had perpetrated this appalling crime, or any of her other classmates, ever again.

Apart from the boys involved, and her father was quite sure they would say nothing, no one else knew what had happened. If they were discreet the terrible incident need never become public knowledge, her parents insisted.

'You won't be staying in Benbury,' her father had said firmly.

'You mean I can go to university and study History!'

'Oh, no! That's out of the question after what has happened. You will have to settle for something more practical, like a business course.'

'Why? I've always dreamed of going to university. You always said I could if I got the right grades.'

'You could have done. But not now, not after what's happened,' her father intervened. He turned to his wife. 'Tell her can't you! Explain why it is pointless to make plans like that,' he said irritably.

Her mother looked uncomfortable. 'It's because of what happened, Maureen. You see, you might be pregnant.'

The shock quelled her ready arguments. It was only much later that she realized how ridiculous it had been to let them take a decision of that kind in the heat of the moment. On the very night she had been raped!

Three months later, when she should have been settling into university, she was both relieved and bitterly aware that they had all worried unnecessarily.

Once they knew she wasn't pregnant her parents' relief was tempered by concern that people might find out what had happened. They made her promise never to talk about the rape ever again, not even to them, and certainly not to anyone outside the family.

And she hadn't. Not until Philip Harmer had been so insistent on knowing all about her past. Then it had come rushing out like wine from an uncorked bottle, gurgling, and spilling, and staining.

By rejecting her because of what had happened all those years ago, Philip Harmer had aroused in her all the rage and resentment she had never expressed as a timid, frightened teenager.

The result had been an intense determination to wreak revenge for the self-hate and sense of inferiority and guilt she'd carried with her all these years.

He'd set in motion a maelstrom that on the one hand terrified her by its implications but on the other filled her with deep-seated satisfaction that the time had come for retribution.

She was determined to exercise all the skills she possessed to create the ultimate in revenge. And then she would put Benbury, and everything pertaining to it, right out of her mind. She would never return. Her whole life would be changed.

It would take time, and concentration, and attention to detail. But she could do it. Tonight had been the first phase, and everything had gone exactly to plan! It had been an unsurpassed success, she congratulated herself.

She finished double-checking everything in the black grip, and then she bundled up the black cagoule, the ultra-sensitive rubber gloves, and the black woolly hat and dropped them into a black bin bag. She slipped off the black canvas trainers she was wearing, which she'd bought only a few days earlier, and dropped them in as well. They'd better go. Better to be safe than sorry.

It was a pity that everything she'd worn wasn't made of paper, then she could have put them through the shredder, she thought as she knotted the top of the black sack. As it was, she'd have to drive to the council tip and dispose of them first thing in the morning.

And then shop for new ones!

It seemed crazy, an unnecessary expense, but all the careful research she had done in advance had made her decide it was imperative. From the many cases she'd studied she was confident that if the people involved had taken this simple precaution of disposing of all the clothes they'd been wearing, right down to their shoes, they would never have been detected.

And the timing, of course. Studying the victim's movements and catching them off guard! That was another prime essential.

It was heady stuff. Like toying with destiny. She had never expected to find it so exciting or so deeply satisfying.

That was probably because everything had gone as smoothly as a well-choreographed dance routine, she told herself.

She let out a deep sigh. She couldn't wait to start working on the next event! Her head was already buzzing with ideas and plans. Common sense warned her that it could be dangerous to be too hasty. There was still a great deal of in-depth research to be done if the second was to be as successful as the first.

She might make a start tonight, after she'd had her bath and cooked herself something special to eat.

She'd been far too keyed up to eat any lunch so now she was ravenous. There was a steak in the fridge. She'd cook that. And since everything had worked out so fantastically successfully, and she felt supremely confident now that nothing could impede her progress, she'd open a bottle of wine as well and really make it a celebration evening.

SIX

Detective Inspector Ruth Morgan and Detective Sergeant Paddy Hardcastle were not the first on the scene.

As soon as Marilyn Moorhouse's 999 call had been put through to the Benbury police, two uniformed men had been sent along to Twenty-Seven Fieldway.

The sight that met them on arrival had been sufficiently horrendous for Sergeant Miller to phone in and ask the duty officer to send the forensic medical officer as well as some additional backup.

'Sounds serious! What are the circumstances?

'John Moorhouse, who is in his mid-thirties, has been stabbed. His clothing is in a most unusual state of disarray. He was discovered by his wife when she brought their two small boys home from Cubs at around eight o'clock. The two boys are now in bed, unaware of what has happened. Mrs Moorhouse is in shock, but reasonably lucid and cooperative.'

'Right. I'll see who is available,' the duty officer promised. 'Hold on there and make a note of anything she may say which might prove useful.'

Sergeant Miller had closed the door of the sitting room, where John Moorhouse's body lay sprawled in an ungainly manner, and left the constable to stand guard just in case a relative or neighbour should turn up and want to go in there.

He persuaded Marilyn Moorhouse, who was looking very white and shaken, to accompany him into the kitchen and suggested that she should make them all a cup of tea.

She nodded, but made no attempt to do anything about it, so he filled the kettle himself, and then switched it on.

'Perhaps you could tell me where you keep the sugar?' he said, after he'd taken down three mugs from one of the shelves, and located a bottle of milk in the fridge.

'I don't take sugar, thank you.'

'No, ma'am. Nor do I. But my constable does.'

Silently, like an automaton, she stood up and crossed the room, opened a cupboard and reached out a container marked 'Sugar', and handed it to him.

While he waited for the kettle to boil, Sergeant Miller tried to make conversation, hoping that she might say something that would indicate what had led to such a terrible tragedy, but although Marilyn Moorhouse appeared to listen to what he was saying she didn't speak a word.

She sat bolt upright on one of the kitchen chairs, staring straight ahead, her blue eyes glassy. She was casually dressed in blue jeans, white trainers and baggy white sweatshirt. It was the sort of outfit a mother of two small boys would be wearing if she'd been with them to Cubs. A small, slight figure with shoulder-length blonde hair, she looked as though the shock of her terrible discovery had left her numbed.

Sergeant Miller felt deeply moved by her traumatized appearance. He, too, felt shocked. Not so much by the fact that John Moorhouse was dead, but by the state he was in. What the hell had been going on for him to be in that sort of predicament when he was stabbed, he wondered.

Marilyn Moorhouse might be your average mum, but what kind of person was her husband? What sort of weird tricks did he get up to when he was on his own?

Since she wasn't saying a word, no matter how hard he tried to get her to open up, did it mean that she had no idea of what had been going on? Alternatively, it could be that she did know, and that she had no intention of discussing it.

Sergeant Miller had just poured out the tea when the plain clothes team arrived. He gave a sigh of relief as he opened the front door to let them in and directed them towards the sitting room.

Although it didn't completely free him from all responsibility, since he had been the first officer on the scene, and therefore technically responsible for taking control, it did mean that he wouldn't have to be the one to try and persuade Marilyn Moorhouse to talk.

Detective Inspector Ruth Morgan, looking slim and efficient in a light-brown suit worn with a crisp white blouse, sheer tan tights, and tan and brown suede flatties, paused in the doorway of the room. Her dark eyes narrowed as she surveyed the body, and her mouth tightened into a thin line.

This was only her second murder case. The first had been fairly straightforward: a shopkeeper who'd been shot when he'd disturbed a thief raiding the safe. The episode had been captured on the security camera, so it had been an open and shut case from the moment of arrest.

This murder was obviously going to be more involved, and she was very conscious that Sergeant Paddy Hardcastle, who'd been assigned to accompany her, was not only ten years older than her, but a seasoned detective.

It was the first time they had worked together, and she was determined to show him that she could handle herself, and the case, like a true professional.

'Has anything in the room been touched?'

'No! Of course not.' Sergeant Miller bristled and shook his head emphatically. Such a question was an insult to his integrity, he thought angrily. DI Morgan surely didn't think he would allow anyone to touch anything before the forensic medical examiner had pronounced John Moorhouse dead and certified the time of death!

He didn't envy Paddy Hardcastle having to work alongside DI Morgan if this was the way she treated subordinates.

She only seemed to be in her late twenties, good-looking and stylish, but he wouldn't mind betting she was a right smarty-pants. These university types were all the same he thought sourly. They might have a briefcase full of qualifications, but they had no hands-on experience whatsoever.

DI Morgan would find she was taking on he wrong man if she thought she could make Paddy Hardcastle jump through any hoops. Paddy had joined the Force the same time as he had, fifteen years ago. They'd trained together, watched each other's backs, and they had both made the rank of sergeant within three months of each other. He'd considered Paddy to be mad when he'd opted for the plain clothes division, but looking back he thought that perhaps Paddy had done the right thing. There appeared to be more to get your teeth into, and it was better than driving round in a panda car all day, acting as nursemaid to new boys, or agony aunt in times of crisis.

Like tonight! Making tea! Sergeant Miller shuddered. He didn't even do that at home. Mind, the poor woman hadn't been in any state to make him a cup of tea, that was for sure.

He'd been to a good number of suicides and murders, but he'd never attended one quite like this. It was the state the poor chap had been left in. Quite disgusting, really. Especially for his wife to find him like that. She seemed such a nice respectable lady.

Still, he reflected, you could never tell what these outwardly proper, middle-class professional types got up to in the privacy of their own homes.

Although outwardly she looked calm, and completely in control, Detective Inspector Ruth Morgan felt her stomach churn as she looked down on the sprawled body of John Moorhouse, and noted the state of disarray of his clothing.

Her immediate reaction was to cover the body over to save his wife from further distress. One swift look in the direction of her sergeant, Paddy Hardcastle, and the procedural training she had so recently undergone at Police College came rushing back into her mind, and restrained her.

Observe, but don't touch when examining the scene of a crime; make careful notes in writing, don't rely on memory; call in specialist officers to take fingerprints and photographs before anything is moved.

She noted that Paddy looked completely unmoved by the shocking sight in front of them. Notebook in hand, he stood his ground squarely. His broad shoulders strained the brown tweed jacket he wore with dark-green trousers, a lemon-coloured shirt, and a tightly-knotted green and brown tie. His handsome, square-jawed face was inscrutable. Only his darting green eyes showed that he was taking an avid interest in every aspect of the room and the people in it as well as the body on the floor.

Paddy was something of a legend, and she had felt some misgivings when he had first been assigned as her sergeant. She'd heard of his reputation and knew he didn't suffer fools gladly. She'd been warned that he was no respecter of rank when it came to plain speaking. And he made no secret of the fact that he held those who had risen from the ranks in much higher regard than those who'd achieved their status by coming into the Force straight from university.

He was also reputed to have one of the keenest brains in the business when it came to detection work, and Ruth was quite prepared to learn from his methods.

Not that she would tell him so! Technically she was the one in charge; even though they both knew she was indisputably dependent on him and his expertise.

Her sympathy was with Marilyn Moorhouse as Paddy began to ply her with questions. His words, though spoken softly, were both probing and barbed. It was almost as if he suspected she might be the one who had murdered John Moorhouse.

'You say you always went out on a Thursday night, Mrs Moorhouse?'

'Yes!' She nodded emphatically. 'It was the night the boys went to Cubs.'

'And you stayed there with them?'

'That's right. I . . . I'm the Cub Mistress.'

'You run the show on your own?'

'Oh, no . . . I simply help out.'

'So who is the Cub Master?'

'Henry Wood.'

Paddy nodded thoughtfully as he made a note of the fact. 'Is this a regular arrangement . . . every Thursday night?

'Yes.'

'Your husband never took part?'

'Oh no. He sees enough of children all day . . .' She hesitated, frowning as though she wondered if it was a trick question. 'I only do it because my two boys Malcolm and Danny belong to the Cub Pack. I thought that since I had to sit and wait for them I might as well help out.'

'So you've done it ever since they joined the Cubs?'

'No. At first I dropped them off, then went to visit a friend for an hour, and then went back and picked them up. After she moved away I decided to stay, and help out.'

Marilyn Moorhouse pushed her long blonde hair back behind her ears in a defensive gesture. 'It seemed madness to drive all the way home and then have to turn straight round to go back to collect them.'

'Yes. Very sensible,' Ruth intervened, trying to take the sting out of Sergeant Hardcastle's questioning. She smiled gently, trying to put Marilyn Moorhouse at ease. 'So there was nothing unusual about tonight?'

'Well, not really except . . .'

'Except? Go on!' Paddy pounced on her brief hesitation.

'The house was in darkness when we got back. I thought John must have fallen asleep.'

'Did he usually take a nap while you were out at Cubs?'

She shook her head. 'I thought perhaps he had a migraine. That was why I stopped the boys going into the sitting room . . .' She dropped her face on to her hands, and a shudder shook her slim shoulders.

'It was as well you did,' murmured Ruth, remembering the sight that had met their eyes on arrival.

The arrival of the forensic medical examiner and the scene of crime officer cut short any further questioning.

Ruth welcomed their intervention. The thought that the children might be wakened by all the commotion, and come downstairs and inadvertently see what had happened to their father, filled her with alarm.

Thankfully, as soon as the FME and SOCO had completed their examination the body could be taken away.

The interval gave Marilyn Moorhouse breathing space to compose herself but Paddy returned to his interrogation the moment they left.

'You were on the point of telling me that you came into the house, went straight into the kitchen, made the boys some supper, and then packed them off to bed.'

'That's right.'

'Before you went to see if your husband was all right?'

Marilyn Moorhouse nodded.

'You weren't curious about why the house was in darkness?'

'I told you! I thought that perhaps John had a migraine.'

'You were quite sure he was here when you arrived home, then?'

'Oh yes! His car was in the garage.'

'And even after you'd put the boys to bed you still didn't go into the sitting room?'

'I thought I would make a pot of tea first, and take it through.'

'And while you were waiting for the kettle to boil you washed up and cleared away the boys' supper things?'

'That's right.'

'You didn't think to put the kettle on before you took them up to bed?' he asked disarmingly. 'That way it would have been boiling when you came back down.'

Marilyn Moorhouse pushed her blonde hair back from her face in a weary gesture. 'I . . . I just didn't think to do that . . .'

'It wasn't because there were other things you wanted to do first . . .' Paddy's voice trailed off.

She shook her head, a bewildered look in her blue eyes.

'You are quite sure?'

'I don't know what you mean.'

'Weren't you terribly angry because your husband had come home, and fallen asleep, while you were taking the boys to cubs?' he said softly. 'Weren't you feeling a little irritated because he hadn't even got supper ready for them, or a cup of tea waiting for you?'

He paused, as if to let his words sink in. When he spoke again his voice was a shade lower and even more intense.

'You were tired out, and yet you were the one who had to prepare their supper, and then see them into bed. And after all that, instead of being able to sit down, and put your feet up, you had to start getting the evening meal ready.'

Marilyn Moorhouse shook her head. 'We never planned anything on Thursday evenings. John liked the chance to have an hour to himself, to relax, listen to music . . .' She stopped, and pressed her hand to her mouth, and Ruth noticed that the look of utter bewilderment was back in her blue eyes, and knew she must intervene.

Sergeant Hardcastle's form of interrogation might be a short cut to extracting a confession, but it wasn't the correct way to go about things. The woman should have her solicitor present, for one thing.

She shot him a glance and was startled to see he was watching her reaction. His own face was impassive. What the hell was he doing? Was he testing her out; pushing his authority to the ultimate just to see how she responded?

Her mouth tightened. Two could play at that game, and she had no intention of letting him use Marilyn Moorhouse as some sort of test case in order to see how she would react to his techniques.

Apart from the ethics involved, Marilyn Moorhouse had gone through quite enough. Finding her husband dead, and in that state, was a sufficiently harrowing experience without being subjected to a third degree.

The arrival of Jim and Peggy Greenside came at a propitious moment. Peggy, a matronly woman in her late forties, explained that she was the dead man's sister, and immediately tried to take charge.

'You can't stay here, Marilyn,' she declared emphatically. 'You and the boys must come back to our place for the night.'

Marilyn shook her head. 'No, Peggy, I can't do that. I don't want to wake the boys . . . I wouldn't know what to tell them,' she protested, her lower lip trembling.

'You can't stay here,' her sister-in-law argued. 'Supposing the murderer came back again!'

Marilyn's blue eyes widened in fear.

'We can leave a uniformed officer on duty,' Ruth told her, 'but I do think it would be better if you did as Mrs Greenside suggests, and went and stayed with her.'

Marilyn Moorhouse's shoulders sagged. She looked as limp as a rag doll inside her bulky white sweatshirt. 'I suppose you're right.'

'Just one point, Mrs Moorhouse . . .' Paddy's voice was diffident. 'Was your husband expecting a visitor this evening?'

'I have no idea. Not as far as I know!'

'I ask because there is no sign of forced entry.'

She looked puzzled. 'Then John must have let him in, I suppose.'

'Him?'

She stared blankly, the colour draining from her face.

'I think perhaps you should collect whatever things you are going to need overnight, Mrs Moorhouse,' Ruth cut in sharply. 'We can discuss this further tomorrow . . . after you've spoken to your solicitor,' she added pointedly.

SEVEN

The atmosphere in the car was as chill as the inside of a fridge as DI Morgan and DS Hardcastle drove back to the station. Ruth suspected that Paddy was annoyed because she had forestalled him asking Mrs Moorhouse any further questions.

Browbeating the witness was not a technique she intended to employ in her enquiries, so she certainly wasn't going to stand quietly by and let him do it, she thought stubbornly.

She shot a sideways glance at him. His large hands were grasping the wheel in an assured, competent way, and he appeared to be concentrating on the traffic ahead, but it was obvious from the set of his broad shoulders, and the tilt of his head, that he was waiting for her to say something.

It needed careful handling. They would be working together for quite some time, and she didn't want to antagonize him. She was well aware that he had probably forgotten more about police procedure than she had learned so far. Even so, she wanted to do things her way. And that didn't include bullying witnesses.

Keeping her voice neutral she remarked, 'Did you think Mrs Moorhouse might have murdered her husband?'

He remained silent long enough to make her feel uncomfortable.

'I always assume everyone is a suspect until proved otherwise,' he commented in an equally impartial tone.

'It could hardly have been her though, could it? There wasn't a spot of blood on her clothes . . .'

'But there was a knife missing from the rack on the kitchen shelf over the right-hand worktop.'

Ruth drew in a quick breath. She should have noticed that, but she hadn't. She didn't intend admitting that to Paddy, though.

'The murder weapon hasn't been found,' she reminded him.

'And until it is, and the forensic tests have been completed, there is no proof that it was the same knife.'

He shrugged but made no comment.

'She didn't look like a woman who had just stabbed her husband half a dozen times in a state of frenzy,' Ruth persisted. 'She was obviously upset but not deranged.'

His mouth twitched, almost as if he was stifling a smile.

Despite herself, Ruth bristled. 'And there was no blood on her clothes,' she repeated almost defiantly when he maintained a solid silence.

'After she'd stabbed him, she could have taken a shower and changed her clothing, before ringing for the police,' he commented in a deceptively soft voice.

'With two small boys upstairs? Don't you think they would have heard the upheaval and come running down to see what was happening?'

'Not if they fell asleep the minute their heads touched the pillow. They'd had a strenuous evening at Cubs, remember.'

'I think if you check out the time of her telephone call, and the time they arrived home, you'll find there wasn't sufficient time for her to do all that.'

'Perhaps she didn't spend the entire evening at Cubs. Supposing after she dropped the boys off, she returned home, murdered her husband, cleaned herself up, and was back in time to collect the two boys, and bring them home as usual.'

'That's a horrific scenario!'

'It could be the reason why she insisted that the boys mustn't go into the sitting room. She knew what was in there.'

'You're making Marilyn Moorhouse out to be not just a murderer, but heartless and cold-blooded into the bargain.'

'If there was another woman involved then she could well have been both those things,' he commented wryly. 'And it accounts for the fact that there was no forced entry.'

'Your theory doesn't hold water, Sergeant Hardcastle.'

'Oh, no? Supposing she suspected that her husband was having an affair, that he was inviting some woman to their home on Thursday nights knowing she was busy with the two boys at Cubs. It would play on her mind. She'd have to find out for herself. So what better way of doing it than sneaking back home again when he thought she was otherwise occupied.'

Ruth shook her head.

'She lets herself in,' Paddy went on, 'she finds her husband with some other woman, and is so incensed that she grabs a knife out of the rack in the kitchen, and stabs him . . .'

'And what does the other woman do! Stand and watch?'

Paddy ignored the interruption. '. . . and stabs him over and over again until her fury is spent. She looks down and sees him lying at her feet in a pool of his own blood. She can't believe what has happened. The other woman has grabbed her clothes and vanished. Marilyn Moorhouse doesn't even remember what she looked like; she certainly doesn't know her. She stands there clutching the knife, blood on her hands, and on her clothes. She strips off, takes a shower, bundles up the clothes, takes a last look at her husband's body, and is too shocked, or too squeamish, to even make sure he looks decent.'

'So she turns out the lights and leaves him lying there while she goes to collect the boys from Cubs?'

Paddy turned and grinned. 'One of us has been reading too many detective stories,' he admonished. 'In real life nothing is as simple as that.'

Ruth felt her colour rising. So he had been winding her up. And what was worse, she had fallen for it. She felt both angry and humiliated. It wasn't a very auspicious start for their partnership, she thought furiously.

'Sorry, ma'am! That was out of order.'

Beneath the seemingly contrite apology, Ruth sensed a tinge of constrained laughter.

'It certainly was, Sergeant,' she agreed stiffly.

Paddy didn't answer. Instead, he slowed down and pulled off the road on to a gravel forecourt. Ruth frowned as she saw the illuminated sign, and realized that they'd pulled into a pub car park.

'Can I buy you a drink, ma'am . . . by way of apology?'

'Well . . .' She was about to refuse, but a sixth sense told her that if she did there would be no possibility of establishing a feeling of comradeship between them.

'We're not in uniform, and technically we've been off-duty

ever since you informed the SOCO that we were leaving
Twenty-Seven Fieldway,' he pointed out.

She bit her lip. It was late. They'd both had a tough evening,
and he was right, they were not wearing uniform, so why
shouldn't she accept his offer, and go for a drink? Perhaps if
she found out what made Sergeant Paddy Hardcastle tick she
would understand him better, and they'd make a better team.

'OK! We'll have a drink . . . only, I'll pay.'

The firmness of her tone surprised her. She shot a quick
sideways glance to gauge his reaction, but the set look on his
square-jawed face gave no inkling of what he was thinking.

A barrage of bright lights and deafening noise met them as
they pushed open the door to the Lounge Bar. It was so packed
that Ruth stepped back. 'Shall we leave it?' she suggested.

'No!' He took her arm, firmly guiding her a few yards along
the building to another door marked Public Bar. Inside it was
quiet and almost empty. A few middle-aged working men were
propping up the bar, a couple of older men ensconced in
armchairs drawn up at a table to one side of the open fire.

'Why don't you find a seat while I get them in,' Paddy
suggested. 'What's your drink, by the way? Lager . . . cider
. . . or a G & T?'

'White wine. Dry if they have it.' She opened her bag, and
took out a note, but he'd already walked away towards the
bar.

She bit her lip and slipped the tenner back inside her bag.
Probably better not to make an issue about paying, she thought
sagely. If things went according to plan, and she was successful
in establishing the right sort of rapport between them, then
there would be plenty of other occasions.

She moved to a corner table and settled on the dark-red
banqueting facing the fire, leaving an armchair for Paddy.
There was enough background noise from the Lounge Bar to
ensure their conversation wasn't overheard.

'I've ordered a couple of rounds of sandwiches,' Paddy told
her as he set down her glass of white wine and a pint of beer
for himself. 'They don't serve meals in here, and I didn't think
you'd want to face the noise in the other bar.'

'You shouldn't have bothered. It might spoil your dinner,' she remarked, checking her watch with the clock over the bar.

'Dinner! What dinner?' He laughed and took a deep draught of his beer. 'Aah, that's better!'

'Surely your wife will have dinner waiting for you?'

'I'm not married!'

'Your mother, then.'

'I live on my own. Self-contained, purpose-built flat with all mod cons. No garden, no pets, just me.'

'That sounds rather lonely.'

He shrugged. 'It suits the hours I keep. More police marriages break up because of the strain of unsociable hours than for any other reason.'

'Is that why you've never married?' she murmured as she took a sip of her wine.

He grimaced. 'Partly. I lived with my mother until she died three years ago. She was a widow, and a semi-invalid. Unsociable hours, and a live-in mother-in-law would be too much to ask any woman to take on, don't you think?'

The arrival of their sandwiches brought a welcome break and saved her from having to comment.

'Help yourself,' he invited. 'There's chicken, beef and cheese.' He grinned. 'I wasn't sure if you were a vegetarian or not.'

The sight of food reminded her how long it was since she'd last eaten. She tucked in, pleasantly surprised at how good the sandwiches were.

'You've eaten here before?'

'Yes. It's my regular. I usually avoid it on Thursday nights because they have a live band playing in the Lounge Bar. That's why it's so packed in there. Other nights it's quite civilized. You'll have to come again sometime. The food is excellent.'

'Only if you let me pay.'

'You're on!' He took another swig of his beer. 'Really into this feminism business, are you?'

'No! I do believe in paying my way, though.'

'Especially when you are in the company of one of your subordinates,' he said with a humourless smile.

'I prefer to think of you as a team-mate not a subordinate,' she told him in a level voice.

His green gaze held hers, and she felt herself colouring.

'Team-mate!' He repeated the phrase as if he was rolling a boiled sweet around in his mouth and testing it for flavour.

She took a deep breath. 'I hope we can work as a team; as partners. You must have a wealth of experience, so I'm sure there's a great deal you can teach me,' she added quietly.

He bit into a sandwich. 'You're the inspector. You're the one who gives the orders, ma'am.'

'Oh, for goodness' sake!' Despite her intention to remain calm, to cajole him into friendship, Ruth found herself exploding with irritation. 'Do you have to call me that? You said yourself we were off duty. If I call you Paddy then surely you can call me Ruth.'

'If those are your orders, ma'am!' His expression was deadpan, but his green eyes gleamed mockingly.

Ruth drained her wine and stood up. 'Can I get you another pint?'

He hesitated, and for a moment she thought he was going to refuse. 'Better make it a half,' he said as he passed his glass to her. 'I'm driving, and a pint might put me over the limit.'

When she returned with their drinks the atmosphere between them seemed to have undergone a positive change.

'Thanks . . . Ruth.' He grinned as she set his beer down in front of him. 'I've told you about my background, and how I live, now how about you telling me something about yourself?'

'Not very different to you. I'm renting a flat, and I live on my own. There didn't seem to be much point in buying a place because I don't know how long I will be in Benbury. If I make a mess of this case I'll probably be moved on very speedily!'

'Which is why you want us to work as a team, so that you can put the blame on me,' he teased.

She shook her head. 'You have so much more practical experience than me that I know I need your fullest cooperation. I've heard the rumours that you had hoped to be promoted to inspector yourself,' she went on, 'so I can understand how you must resent me being brought in over your head, and put in charge. I know I would have felt resentful if I'd been in your shoes,' she told him.

He passed a hand through his thick fair hair, averting his eyes. 'And what would you have done about it?'

She shrugged. 'The same as you, I expect. Made the best of things.'

His green eyes narrowed. 'So that's what you hope I'm going to do, is it?'

She nodded. 'I hope so. It would be best for both of us if you did.'

He helped himself to the one remaining sandwich and chewed it thoughtfully. 'Yes, you're right,' he admitted. 'I knew I didn't stand a chance of being made up to inspector. Not the right sort of background or handshake, for one thing.'

She grinned. 'I suppose university did help, but I don't know about the handshake.'

He took a drink of his beer. 'I've my own way of doing things, and I don't go along with a lot of theorizing, and all this psychological stuff. I'm a practical man who prides himself on being able to sum up people pretty accurately.'

'By pressurizing them into admitting things they might have done, or you would have liked them to have done, like you did with Marilyn Moorhouse?' she asked.

He chuckled, and drained his glass. 'No, that was a bit out of order, but I was keen to find out your reaction.'

'I wasn't the one being subjected to your third degree.'

'Why did you join the police?'

'Personal reasons.'

He looked at her in silence for a moment. 'Are you telling me to mind my own business?'

'No, not really. I really did join for personal reasons. My young brother was on a murder charge. The whole family knew he was innocent, but we had no proof. He was on remand for months. I was in my teens, and as I watched the struggle to clear his name I became fascinated by police procedure . . .'

'So why didn't you become a lawyer when you left university?'

'I wanted to be one of the first on the scene so that I could be sure that justice was being done, not sitting in an office having evidence presented to me second-hand.'

Paddy nodded approvingly. 'Well said!' He stood up to leave. 'Maybe we can be partners after all,' he added, holding out his hand.

EIGHT

Maureen Flynn knew quite well that it was utter madness returning to Benbury so soon after John Moorhouse's murder, but she was drawn back there as a wasp is to a glass of beer.

Sitting in the cafe opposite the newsagent's she studied the poster clipped on to the display stand outside the shop.

BENBURY SCHOOLTEACHER DIES IN
MYSTERIOUS CIRCUMSTANCES.
NO CLUES TO KILLER OF POPULAR
BENBURY TEACHER.

As she studied it, reading it over and over again as if mesmerized, she saw the rangy figure of Sandy Franklin come out of the shop, and she held her breath as he slipped a new sheet into the frame.

POLICE STILL SEEKING CLUES
TO THE IDENTITY OF
BENBURY TEACHER'S ATTACKER.

Maureen found herself gritting her teeth as she watched him smile and speak to every woman who passed by. If they stopped, not content with jocular exchanges, he would pat them on the shoulder, grasp them by the arm, or slip his hand around their waist, and her hatred for him surged afresh as she observed his antics.

He should have been her first victim, she mused. What Sandy Franklin had done to her all those years ago had been far worse than John Moorhouse's involvement.

Seething with mindless rage, Maureen pushed aside her coffee, picked up her handbag, and went out into the street. Her throat felt so tight that she could hardly breathe, and once outside on the pavement she gulped greedily at the fresh air.

Her heart hammered as she saw Sandy Franklin look in her direction, and she was rooted to the spot as he started to cross the road. For a split second she thought he had recognized her and that he was coming to speak to her.

Then she noticed that a silver-coloured Mercedes coupé had pulled up almost alongside her. The female driver, a heavily made-up blonde wearing a low cut black sweater, and a skimpy red skirt that had ridden high up her thighs, had wound down the window, and was smiling up at him.

Oblivious to the fact that people were watching them, Sandy Franklin stopped in the middle of the road, and bent down towards the woman, who reached up and pulled his head closer so that they could kiss.

'Am I seeing you tonight?' she asked as he straightened up.

'Do you want to, Tracey?'

The woman's heavily pencilled eyebrows rose invitingly. 'What do you think, big boy?'

'Eight o'clock? Your place?' queried Sandy Franklin.

The woman flashed a wide smile, revved her car engine, and let out the clutch, leaving him standing in the middle of the road.

As Maureen walked back to the car park near the library where she'd left her Ford Escort, anger, contempt and hatred battled inside her. Sandy Franklin had not only been one of the instigators when she'd been raped, he had enjoyed every minute inside the horrible dark shed. He'd goaded the others into action, forcing John Moorhouse to take part when he'd hung back, and he'd gone along with all the vile suggestions Dennis Jackson had made. He'd been slobbering with excitement when it came to his turn.

Her mind alive with memories, she drove round and round Benbury for almost two hours, visiting the haunts of her childhood, reliving the past. It was as though she was watching a video over and over again.

She knew she should be heading back to Dutton. It was over an hour's drive, and there was really nothing to keep her in Benbury any longer.

Or was there? Could she return home without first eradicating the ghost of Sandy Franklin from her thoughts?

She decided to drive down the High Street one last time before she went home. Most of the shops were now closed. A few of them had left lights on so that passers-by could view their window displays, but the rest were in darkness, with only a safety light over the till.

The lights were still on in the newsagent's. Maureen slowed to a crawl as she toyed with the idea of going in and confronting Sandy Franklin. It would be so satisfying to see his face when she reminded him who she was.

Do that and you have as good as owned up to John Moorhouse's murder, she told herself. Sandy Franklin will phone the police right away, and when he tells them what he knows about you then without doubt you'll be the chief suspect.

Unless I stop him from using the phone. Not only now . . . forever!

The idea appealed to her.

And why not! She'd come prepared! Not intentionally, of course. It had just happened that way.

She'd stopped at Castleton for lunch, and afterwards had decided to walk around the new shopping precinct there. She was surprised at how large it was, and had decided she might as well take the opportunity to replace the items she had destroyed after her confrontation with John Moorhouse.

It had been a surprisingly successful buying spree. All the new items were now stowed away in the boot of her car in readiness for when she might need them.

Outside Sandy Franklin's newsagent's she switched off the engine and undid her seat belt. She was about to get out of her car when she saw that although all the lights were still blazing there was a 'CLOSED' notice on the door.

She hesitated. He was in there. She could see him. He was standing by the till cashing up. She wondered if he would come to the door if she knocked. Or would he think it was a burglar and phone the police?

Why should he do that when he could see who was at the door, she reasoned. He would be able to see it was a woman, and probably assume she wanted cigarettes, or a magazine, or sweets or something, point to the 'Closed' sign, and wave her away.

Or would he? A woman on her own. Would he be able to resist letting her into the shop and making a pass at her?

While she dithered, the lights inside the shop suddenly went out, leaving only a small red alarm light shining over the till.

Biting her lip in disappointment, Maureen remained in her car. She sat there, fingers drumming on the steering wheel, wondering what to do. She looked up as a light went on in one of the windows above the shop. She supposed he must live there.

She looked at her watch. It was quarter to eight. Sandy Franklin had an appointment to meet his blonde lady friend at eight o'clock!

She was still debating whether or not to wait until he came out when a long dark car emerged from the covered way at the side of the shop and turned left down the High Street.

Within seconds Maureen was following the sleek dark Jaguar, hoping she would be able to keep up with it since it was three times as powerful as her own car.

Left, right, then left again, and they were on the river road. It was a part of Benbury she remembered from her childhood; magical days when, carrying a brown paper bag of bread, she had been taken there to feed the ducks.

The car in front braked suddenly, and then turned into the forecourt of a block of luxury apartments, nosing its way into a slot between a Porsche and a Saab.

Maureen stopped in the road outside, wondering what to do next. She could hardly turn in and park alongside the Mercedes, Rovers, BMWs and Jaguars. Her Ford would look as out of place as a mongrel at a pedigree dog show.

She drove on down the road a little way, parked by the curb, and walked back along the lamplit road.

There was no one about. On one side of her the river, black and mysterious, whispered gently against its banks. Leaning against the iron railings that stretched like a protective barrier between the river and the pavement, Maureen studied the block of flats.

Accrington Court. Very nice! And this was where Sandy Franklin's lady friend, Tracey, lived!

It was certainly impressive. Huge picture windows, patio doors on to a balcony large enough to take two chairs, and a small table. It would be an idyllic place to sit and relax with a drink in hand and watch what was happening on the river.

There were lights showing in most of the living room windows. Some of the occupants hadn't drawn their curtains. She watched them moving around. A woman was laying a table, a man switching on the television. In another, drink in hand, a man was walking towards the window.

Maureen felt a moment's panic. Could he see her? If so, he would be wondering what she was doing out there in the dark, staring up at his window. She walked towards the flats, hoping that if he had seen her he'd think she was a visitor.

As she crossed the forecourt, Maureen felt drawn towards Sandy Franklin's car. She went over to it, peering into the interior. There were no traces of ownership. Not even a briefcase, or a discarded jacket, on the back seats.

She walked briskly across to the porticoed entrance to the flats where there was a board containing the names of the occupiers. She studied it, wishing she knew the woman's surname. Hardly likely to have Tracey written on the board!

Then she spotted it. There it was! Tracey Walker, flat Sixteen. That must be the Tracey he was visiting. No Mr Walker listed. Did that mean she wasn't married?

Mulling over what she had discovered, she retraced her steps across the courtyard to the road outside and tried to work out which one was number sixteen.

Shivering with the cold, she went back to her own car for a jacket. The first thing she saw when she opened the boot were the clothes she'd bought in Castleton. Warm jogging bottoms, a black cagoule and comfortable trainers. It made sense to change into them.

She walked up and down the pavement, always keeping the apartment block in sight. Each time she walked past the forecourt she took the precaution of checking that Sandy Franklin's car was still parked there.

She knew it was crazy, but she felt compelled to wait. She was confident that he would be out soon. He wouldn't stay the night; as a newsagent he would have to be up so early.

No woman would want her lover leaving before dawn. Not Tracey, she'd bet on that. Tracey would send him packing before she settled for the night.

There was hardly anyone about. Now and again a couple would wander by, hand in hand, eyes only for each other.

The March evening darkened as clouds gathered bringing cold, slanting rain. Maureen refused to abandon her vigil.

All I have to do is be patient, she told herself.

Sandy Franklin wasn't looking forward to his evening with Tracey Walker. His mind was made up. Tracey had become far too demanding. They'd had some great times together, he'd enjoyed their fling, but enough was enough. The time had come to put an end to their relationship.

Tom Walker had been a business contact. A pompous, pot-bellied, magazine wholesaler. A bald-headed, cigar-smoking workaholic who'd worshipped the ground Tracey walked on, and paraded her like a kid with a Barbie-doll.

While Tom was alive, Sandy had been quite happy with their arrangement. Tracey had been as keen as he was to conceal their affair. The minute Tom keeled over from a heart-attack, though, she'd been so brazen-faced about seeing him that Sandy had felt embarrassed.

Enamoured though he was by Tracey, Tom had never taken the trouble to change his will. Nor had he made Tracey his wife. She had simply taken the name Walker after they'd moved into Accrington Court. And when Tom Walker died, his entire estate went to Agnes Walker, his legal wife.

Tracey's anger had far outweighed her grief. She'd been so incensed that she'd shouted the details from the rooftop.

Sandy suspected that she saw him as a substitute for Tom Walker. Someone who as well as being her lover would provide her with a comfortable home and all the money she needed to maintain the lifestyle she'd grown used to.

Sandy didn't see things that way at all. Each time she broached the subject of moving in with him he'd skilfully managed to dissuade her.

'Living over a newsagent's would cramp your style after Accrington Court,' he'd said with a laugh.

Tracey had shrugged her shapely shoulders and tried to look soulful. 'We'd be together, sweetie, and that's what matters. Anyway, I won't be able to stay here much longer. The lease expires in a month's time.'

'The lease?'

'Tom didn't own the place, silly!'

'He only leased it!'

She pouted. 'Don't make it sound so awful. He already had a mortgage on his family home.'

'Where Agnes lives?'

'That's right.'

'And Agnes doesn't know about this place?'

Tracey shrugged. 'Probably not. I don't know. Tom took out the lease in my name. He paid all the bills . . .'

'So at the end of the month, when the lease expires, you'll have to get out?'

Tracey nodded dejectedly.

'And you've nowhere to go?'

Tracey smiled up at him expectantly, waiting for him to come up with a solution.

Sandy looked away. If she thought she could move in with him then she was going to be disappointed. That was the last thing he wanted.

Spending two, or at the most three, nights a week with Tracey was more than enough.

He had other fish in his little pond, some of them a great deal younger than Tracey. He liked living on his own. That way he could entertain whoever he wanted, whenever he wanted.

And not only girls!

He couldn't see Tracey accepting that. And if she did, she might try to muscle in and spoil his fun.

Sandy suppressed a shiver. Ditching her wasn't going to be easy, he thought, remembering the day Tom Walker had died. He'd suggested then to Tracey that they should cool things between them for a little while, until her friends had time to accept that she had overcome her grief. Then they could renew their relationship without any chance of scandal. Her comment had shocked even him.

'Bugger what they think! He's dead and I'm still alive. No point in sitting around mourning. That won't bring him back. Not that I'd want him back, anyway. Boring old fart!'

As Tracey's lips curved contemptuously, what had been merely a vague uneasy thought in Sandy Franklin's mind until then became a matter of urgency. His peccadilloes might be known to some of his closest friends, who shared the same kind of preferences, but to all outward appearances he was a respectable business man, and he wanted to keep it that way.

When she'd driven down the High Street earlier that day and hailed him so publicly, he'd wanted to clamp a hand over her mouth not kiss her. He'd agreed to meet her that night so that he could tell her it was all over between them.

He didn't believe in prolonging the agony over things like this. Say what had to be said and get it over with.

She'd be livid, of course. He was pretty sure she'd make a scene, which was why he didn't want to tell her in public, and why the privacy of her flat seemed to be the best place to sever their acquaintance.

Far from depressing him, the thought that once it was done she would never speak to him again, and that she would be out of his life for good, filled him with relief.

NINE

'This' is the second murder on your patch in as many weeks. What are you doing about it?'

Detective Superintendent Wilson's voice was harsh. He placed both his arms on the massive teak desk and leaned forward in an almost menacing manner.

On the other side of the desk, Detective Inspector Ruth Morgan and Detective Sergeant Paddy Hardcastle sat to attention, feeling as vulnerable as two children facing the headmaster.

'We've only had time to do a preliminary enquiry on the second murder . . .'

'The one at Accrington Court?'

'Yes, sir.'

'And?'

Ruth resisted the impulse to shrug her slim shoulders, suspecting that if she did so it would only make her superior even angrier than he was already.

'Like the first murder, sir, there are no clues, no eyewitnesses, and very little information to go on.'

'Have you no theories? Do you think it's the handiwork of the same person?'

'Possibly! It's hard to tell.'

Superintendent Wilson scowled. 'You do understand that if it is the same person then you have a serial killer on your hands.'

'Yes, sir.'

'Both victims are highly respectable citizens, so you'd better find out damn quick who the killer is.'

'Yes, sir. We intend to do so.'

'Intend! That's not good enough, Inspector. I want action and I want it immediately.' Superintendent Wilson's scowl deepened. 'If it is the same killer then this second murder should never have happened.' He shot a keen glance at

Detective Sergeant Paddy Hardcastle. 'What is your opinion?'

'Like DI Morgan says, it is quite possible that it is the same person, sir. Identical *modus operandi*. Very clever operator. Whoever it is pays meticulous attention to detail. No fingerprints, no clues . . .'

'But the same weapon. A kitchen knife . . . yes?'

'That's right, sir. But not the same knife. The knife used in this second murder had a slightly wider blade.'

'Multiple stabbing, though? Exactly the same as the first time.'

'That's correct, sir.'

'Have you established whether the two men were friends or not?'

'Not that we can discover. John Moorhouse, the man who was murdered first, was a teacher. He probably knew Sandy Franklin because Franklin had a newsagent's shop in the High Street and—'

'Yes, yes, yes!' interrupted Superintendent Wilson testily. 'I'm quite sure he knew Franklin. We all know Franklin. Everyone in Benbury goes into his shop at some time or the other. It's the only place in Benbury selling lottery tickets.'

The interview, half probing, half dismissive of what they had so far achieved, went on for almost an hour.

'I think we both need a coffee after that,' breathed Paddy when they finally emerged from the superintendent's office.

Ruth shook her head. 'You go. I want to get back to my office and record the finer points of this meeting while they're still etched on my mind.'

'Surely, that's not necessary!'

She managed a faint smile. 'It is to me. Superintendent Wilson has such a regimented way of thinking. Come to my office when you've had your coffee; I should be through by then.'

Paddy grinned. 'I'll do better than that. I'll pop down to the canteen and get us both a coffee, and bring them back to your office.' He was gone before she could protest.

She was studying a printout of details relating to the latest murder when Paddy arrived with their coffee.

'Solved it?' he asked jokingly, putting her cup down on a pile of papers

She frowned. 'Far from it!'

'What's the problem?'

'The fact that Sandy Franklin was known to such a wide range of people in Benbury.'

He took a gulp of his coffee. 'Why is that such a complication?'

'It means that absolutely anyone could have murdered him!'

Paddy shook his head. 'No one is going to murder him because he's short-changed them or been late delivering their papers. Whoever did it must have a real grudge against him, probably a strong personal one. He was a bit of a lad with the ladies, you know!'

Ruth checked her notes. 'A bachelor. Living on his own . . .'

'Who liked a good time and female company.'

'You mean it could have been a jealous husband?'

'It's quite possible.'

'And from his reputation that also means there could be more than one suspect?'

'Yes, that's more than likely.'

Ruth picked up her mug of coffee. 'So we need to find out the names of his lady friends.' She took a drink. 'Have you any suggestions?'

'Not at the moment, but I'm sure that Franklin's cleaner, Betsy Grey, would be able to tell us all we want to know.'

Ruth nodded thoughtfully. 'Perhaps you should pop along and have a chat with her. That is, if you think she would be helpful.'

'Catch her at the right moment, and she'd open up. She's a widow in her mid-fifties and very fond of drinking a G & T in the Red Lion.'

Ruth's eyebrows lifted slightly. 'Right! Well, I'll leave you to take care of that line of enquiry. I'm sure you won't mind dropping in there on your way home.' She scanned another sheet of paper. 'None of the staff at his shop appear to have been very helpful.'

'No. They're all part-timers. They do their hours and then

they're off. They've no real interest in him, or the business, from what I could gather.'

'And the delivery boys?'

Paddy shrugged. 'The same. In the morning, their main concern is to get their deliveries over and be at school on time. At night, they want to be finished as quickly as possible and go home.'

'I think we ought to find out what clubs, or other organizations, Sandy Franklin belonged to, and check if John Moorhouse was a member of any of the same ones.'

'You think there is a connection?'

'The two murders are almost identical. That could mean that it's a copycat murder. If not, then, as Superintendent Wilson said, it might well be that we have a serial killer on our hands.'

Paddy drained the dregs of his coffee. There were plenty of rumours flying around about who might have murdered Sandy Franklin, but he didn't think it was his place to mention them. He wasn't sure if she would approve of gossip.

If it had been Inspector Ben Palmer on the case that would have been a very different matter, because he would have known exactly where he stood with old Ben.

Paddy sighed. A damn sight easier dealing with a seasoned copper like himself who had worked his way up from the beat and had real practical experience.

He liked DI Morgan well enough, but he still thought it was all wrong the way she had been made inspector because she had a university degree. Here he was, nudging forty, and with twenty years' experience of police work to draw on. Ten years on the beat, before being promoted to sergeant; then four years on traffic, before a sideways move into the plain clothes division two years ago.

Give Ruth Morgan another five years, and she'd probably be up to superintendent, breathing fire at her junior ranks the same as Detective Superintendent Wilson was doing now.

And, in all probability, Paddy reflected, I'll still be a sergeant!

It wasn't altogether a criticism of Ruth, he told himself; it was the system. As a person, he quite liked her. A bit prim and proper, but then she was not only nearly twenty years younger than him but new on the job and probably afraid of putting a foot wrong.

All that talk about team work, and being partners, that she'd spouted the night he'd persuaded her to have a drink on their way back from the Moorhouse murder must have been the wine talking. Twice since then she'd refused to go for a coffee with him.

It wasn't as though they were in uniform! If they went into a café, who would know that she was his boss? Most people would think they were friends meeting for a chat. Still, if that was the way she wanted to play things then he'd have to go along with it. She was his boss.

Give her a few more months and she might ease up. Two murders one after the other was a big one for her to cut her teeth on. He just hoped she realized how lucky she was to have someone with his experience to guide her through it.

All this talk about Sandy Franklin's murder being a copycat one, or that they had a serial killer on their hands, was all theoretical textbook stuff, in his opinion. More likely it was merely a coincidence that both murders had occurred in a space of a week, and that in both instances the same type of weapon had been used. There hadn't had a murder in Benbury for at least five years, which was probably why it was scaring the pants off old Wilson.

What the super hadn't mentioned – and which in all probability Ruth didn't know either, since she hadn't referred to it – was that Sandy Franklin was a Mason, and so was the superintendent. Paddy didn't know for sure, but he'd bet any money you liked that they were in the same lodge. Which was why the super was so anxious to apprehend the murderer. As soon as he had the chance, he'd check out if John Moorhouse had also been a Mason. If so, then, and only then, would he mention this fact to Ruth. In the meantime, there were plenty of routine enquiries to be carried out, starting with Sandy Franklin's numerous lady friends.

'Perhaps we should resume our enquiries at Accrington Court,' Ruth commented, breaking into his reverie. 'Franklin must have been visiting someone there since his car was parked on their private forecourt.'

'Whoever it was obviously wasn't interested in helping the police with their enquiries or they'd have come forward as soon as the body was found.'

'There are only twenty-four flats in the block, so door-to-door enquiries shouldn't take long. Come on, we'll make it top priority.'

No one actually shut the door in their faces, they were much too well-bred for that, but most of the residents made it quite obvious that they were reluctant to get involved.

Two hours later, however, they had established that Sandy Franklin was a frequent visitor to Accrington Court. Several people confirmed that he came there three or even four times a week to visit Mrs Tracey Walker at Flat Sixteen.

There was no reply from Flat Sixteen, and no one in the adjacent flats had seen her since the night Franklin had been murdered, or could offer any suggestions as to where she might be.

They returned to the office feeling more than a little disgruntled. The name Walker rang a bell, Paddy admitted. Someone of that name had died only a couple of months ago and there had been some sort of dispute over the will.

'And you think there may be some sort of connection?'

'I remember!' His handsome face lit up. 'Tom Walker. He was a magazine wholesaler. Of course he would know Sandy Franklin. He'd have been one of his suppliers, and they'd have met at trade functions.'

'Anything else?'

Paddy chewed on his lower lip. 'Yes! I remember now. I had occasion to speak to Tracey Walker once when I was in Traffic Division. She'd overstayed on a restricted parking area. A very sexy blonde piece! Nice smile. I remember I let her off with a caution. She'd be very much Sandy Franklin's type.'

'Tom Walker is dead, you say?'

'That's right. He died quite suddenly, a couple of months back . . .'

'Which means he couldn't have done it.'

'True.' He looked thoughtful. 'And I don't think she'd be the type . . . Still, you never know. We probably ought to bring her in for questioning.'

'We have to find her first. If you remember, she wasn't at home and no one seemed to know where she might be.'

'We could start with Walker's wife and see what she can tell us.'

'I thought this Tracey was his wife?'

Paddy chuckled. 'That's what everyone in Benbury thought until Tom Walker's will was read. Then it came out that he was merely living with Tracey. She'd taken his name, but he already had a wife. Tracey raised an outcry because he'd left all his money to his legal wife.'

'Almost a reason for murder in itself, except that Tom Walker is already dead,' murmured Ruth dryly. 'So where does Sandy Franklin fit into this little triangle?'

Paddy hesitated. 'Rumour has it . . .'

Ruth went on as if thinking aloud. 'He could have gone there to offer her some advice . . .'

'And she lost her temper and stabbed him? I suppose it's possible, but not very likely.'

'Tom Walker's wife might have gone to Accrington Court to see Tracey, to have things out with her about the slanderous things Tracey was saying about her. and found Franklin there.'

'And killed him in a fit of pique because she'd always thought of him as a friend of her husband's and was outraged to find him visiting Tracey?'

Ruth shook her head. 'I think that's rather far-fetched.'

'Think about it. Even a worm turns . . . in time. And she had recently lost her husband, remember. Grief can affect people's minds in the strangest ways.'

'I think you are grasping at straws, or you've been listening to too much local gossip,' Ruth told him crisply.

Paddy shrugged. 'Perhaps you're right.'

'I hope so, otherwise it means we really are looking for two murderers, since there couldn't possibly be any connection between Franklin's death and that of John Moorhouse if it was the result of a love triangle.'

TEN

Detective Superintendent James Wilson was not in the best of moods. It had been a long evening, and he had far more pressing matters on his mind than instructing Brian Patterson on what his duties would be when he became master at their next meeting.

For a solicitor, he ruminated, Patterson was exceedingly apprehensive about what he was taking on. He supposed it went with his profession – all this cross-questioning and repeating, and checking whatever he was told.

Silently, he admonished himself to be patient. At least it would relieve some of the pressure from his shoulders once Brian was installed. He'd so much on his plate at the moment. Not least these two murders.

As if reading his mind, Brian switched from talking about his own forthcoming induction to commenting on what had been happening in Benbury over the past few weeks.

Wilson braced himself. At the lodge meeting they'd both attended he'd been in the unenviable position of telling his fellow Masons that one of their members had met with an untimely death, so it was inevitable that the matter was upper-most in Patterson's mind.

It had been doubly unpleasant making the announcement because everyone knew that, as detective superintendent in Benbury, he was in charge of the case. He'd found it extremely embarrassing having to admit that up to the time of speaking, no one had been apprehended. Even so, he was surprised at how upset Brian Patterson was over Sandy Franklin's death.

'He was one of my clients as well as a fellow Mason,' Brian confided. 'I've known him all my life . . . We were at school together!'

James Wilson's steely grey eyes registered surprise. It was hard to think of the thin, balding little man standing alongside him as a schoolboy or a contemporary of Franklin's . . . or as

one of his friends. Sandy Franklin had been brash and
boisterous, with a forceful outgoing personality. Patterson
looked years older than Franklin and had the character of a
grisly old ferret.

James Wilson was used to having big burly men around
him most of the time, and he felt a revulsion he found hard
to disguise for the prim little man in his chalk-striped navy
suit and ghastly polka-dot bow tie.

Furthermore, he detested Patterson's habit of constantly
rubbing his hands together so ingratiatingly. And the way
Patterson peered from behind his pebble-lenses, gave him the
creeps.

It had been his opinion that Sandy Franklin, not Patterson,
should have been the one stepping into his shoes as master,
but he'd been overruled because of Sandy's reputation.

The problem had been that Sandy Franklin fancied himself
as a ladies' man, and several of the members bore a deep-seated
grudge because, in the past, he'd been more than friendly with
their wives.

'Oh yes, we were at school together,' repeated Brian
Patterson. 'In fact in the same class as John Moorhouse. And
Dennis Jackson, the estate agent. You probably know him. I
act for him, too, and I was only saying to him today . . .'

Wilson let his thoughts stray to more important matters as
the garrulous reminiscences flowed. At the first opportunity he
cut across Patterson's diatribe. Glancing down at his Rolex
he exclaimed in a falsely surprised voice, 'Heavens! Is that the
time? I must be going.'

'I'll walk across to your car with you. There are still one
or two points I want to check out,' Patterson murmured
anxiously.

Controlling his irritation, Wilson nodded, and they left the
hall together. It had been raining earlier in the evening, and
the tarmac glistened damply underfoot as they made their way
to the car park. The sky, still banked with clouds, had an eerie
green tinge as the moon struggled to make an appearance from
behind them.

'I'm parked over by the gate,' stated Wilson, and began to
stride purposefully in that direction. 'Where's your car?'

'Oh, I'm round at the back of the hall. I was one of the first to arrive, and I always feel my car is least likely to get a knock if I park there. Most of the chaps have company cars, but I have to buy mine myself, and so I take doubly good care of it.'

Wilson barely paused. 'Right. I'll say goodnight then.'

'I'll walk you to your car,' insisted Patterson. 'As I said, there's still a couple of things I want to ask you. We rather got carried away talking about Sandy Franklin! Still, you know how it is when it's one of your boyhood friends.'

His voice was so obsequiously oily that Wilson shuddered in distaste as he unlocked his Rover and tossed the leather case containing his Masonic regalia on to the passenger seat. Sliding in behind the wheel, he lowered the window and once more bid Patterson goodnight.

'Now, you're quite sure you've told me everything I need to know . . .'

'Absolutely! You'll carry everything off perfectly,' Wilson assured him.

'There are one or two small points . . .'

'Stop worrying!' Wilson switched on the engine and began slowly backing the car out. 'Believe me, everything will be fine!'

Brian Patterson nodded reluctantly. 'Well, I can see you're in a hurry. I'll phone you if there is anything else I need to know.'

He was still standing in the middle of the empty parking area when Superintendent James Wilson drove out of the gateway.

Watching him in his rear mirror, Wilson once again felt that it was hard to believe that Patterson and Franklin were the same age. Patterson looked at least ten years older.

Perhaps it had something to with their personalities. Patterson always had such a shifty look about him. It was as though he had the worries of the world on his shoulders, or as if he was trying to hide some deep dark secret.

A man less likely to be a solicitor would be hard to find, James Wilson thought as he nosed his way into the late night traffic and headed for home.

*   *   *

Brian Patterson's head was filled with a dense tangle of intertwining thoughts as he watched James Wilson drive away. He couldn't understand why Wilson hadn't been more impressed by the fact that he had been at school with both John Moorhouse and Sandy Franklin.

He'd half hoped that Wilson would question him, delve into the past a bit. That would have given him a chance to voice the disquiet that had been nagging at him all week.

He had a more analytical mind than most people, he reflected. And an incredibly reliable memory for dates and events. He put that down to his training, and the fact that he'd been practising as a solicitor for almost twelve years.

A great many of the things he remembered from his own past didn't reveal him in a very good light, and he would have preferred to forget them. Nothing criminal, merely incidents which gnawed at his conscience, from time to time, and tormented him. He deplored his own foolhardiness. Probably, he worried too much.

Perhaps he should have been more like Sandy Franklin: taken it all in his stride and freed himself from the grip of the past. He even found himself dwelling on a misdemeanour from his schooldays. By now he should have put that out of his mind. After all, it had only been a high-spirited boyhood prank, and what was done couldn't be undone, no matter however much you might regret it.

He had plenty of clients who could vouch for that. One slip could change the entire pattern of your life, if you let it! As he walked across to his car he speculated on whether a man ever fully controlled his own destiny.

He sighed. So often it was other people's actions that involved you in a situation from which there was no escape.

Bill Smart stubbed out his cigarette, and then he made one last round of the Masonic Hall, checking that all the doors were closed in case a fire should break out in the night.

His last call was to the cloakroom to make sure that no one had left anything behind. It always amazed him that they could go off without their scarf, or gloves, or briefcases. Easy come easy go, he supposed. If they lost them then they'd simply go out and buy new ones.

Not like him and Elsie. They had to watch every penny, especially since the factory where he'd worked for over thirty years had closed down.

When he'd been made redundant he'd thought that was the end. It had been a stroke of luck landing this caretaking job. It didn't pay much, only about half what he'd been earning before, but Elsie had found a part-time job at the newsagent's in the High Street, and that helped.

Another three years and they'd both be drawing their state pension. That wasn't a fortune either, but at least it came in regular each week. With any luck they'd keep him on as caretaker. Just as long as he did a good job.

Satisfied that everyone had gone home, he locked and bolted the huge oak entrance doors and went out of the small side door that led into the back car park, making sure he double-locked that behind him.

It was then that he saw there was still a car parked over by the far wall.

'I wonder why he's still here?' he muttered aloud.

'What's the trouble? Won't she start?' he called out as he walked over to see if he could help.

The figure leaning over the bonnet neither answered nor stirred.

Bill Smart felt puzzled. Something was wrong. The man was lying face down. Bill wondered if he'd been doing something to his windscreen and then collapsed with a heart attack. By now Bill Smart was right alongside the car, near enough to touch the man. He spoke again, but there was no movement.

Perhaps I ought to check if he's still breathing, he thought, and moved closer to do so.

His own heart started to pound, and the back of his neck prickled. He didn't know what to do for the best. Situations like this unnerved him completely. Perhaps he should nip back into the Hall and phone for an ambulance.

He looked around. The car park was deserted. Away in the distance he could hear the traffic in the main road. His instinct was to get out fast and forget what he'd seen, but that wouldn't hold up if he was questioned. It was part of his duties to check the car park each night. He couldn't say someone must have got in after he'd left because the last thing he was supposed to do before leaving was make sure everyone *had* left, and then lock the gates.

Stuffing his hands in his pockets to make quite sure he didn't accidentally touch anything and leave incriminating fingerprints, Bill Smart bent down and peered more closely.

The man was lying face downwards, and there was a scraper in his hand. It looked as though he'd been cleaning his windscreen and then been attacked from behind.

Bill's bowels went weak as he saw that the knife the killer had used was still there!

The handle was sticking out midway between the victim's shoulders. There was a dark stain on the back of his overcoat, and there was something wet all over the bonnet of the car. It must be blood, Bill decided as it shone glassily in a beam of light from the street lamp in the next road.

Taking great care not to touch it or let it come in contact with his own clothes, Bill bent his head to one side and studied the man's profile.

He was shocked to find that it was Mr Patterson, the solicitor. He knew Patterson all right – thin faced, pebble-glasses, going bald. Bit of a busybody. Always telling him what he should and should not do. He would be even more officious next year when he was master.

Bill Smart drew in a sharp breath. Mr Patterson wouldn't be master though . . . not now.

He straightened up, wondering what to do next. Patterson looked dead, but he supposed he ought to make sure. Tentatively, he took one of his hands out of his pocket and placed it on the man's forehead then pulled back sharply. The moist coldness sent a shudder through him.

No point in sending for an ambulance . . . or trying to revive him, he decided. Yet he had to do something. He couldn't leave him lying there. For one thing he needed the car park clear so that he could lock up for the night.

Still not too sure about what was the right action to take, he went back into the Masonic Hall to phone the police.

He'd better phone Elsie as well, he decided. She'd be worrying as it was because he was late. By the time the police arrived, and he'd answered all their questions, it might be another hour before he could get home.

When Elsie answered the phone the implication of what had happened, and of what he had seen, hit him afresh. His voice shook as he explained why he was going to be late.

'Here, Bill, are you all right? You sound quite shaky. Would you like me to come and be there with you?'

'No, no. You stay where you are!' The thought of her seeing Patterson's body with a knife sticking out of his back horrified him.

'Well, if you're quite sure you're all right . . .'

'Yes, yes. Nothing at all for you to worry about. I only phoned to let you know I'll be a bit late in case you were worried when I wasn't home at my usual time. I've phoned the police. They told me to wait here. They'll be along soon.'

'Very well, then, Bill. If you think you can manage. I must say I don't like it though.'

In some strange way, Elsie's concern helped to restore Bill's confidence.

'I'll be OK. Now, don't you worry. Just keep my meal hot till I get home.'

'Yes, I'll do that,' she promised. 'It's most upsetting, though. This means now that there's been three murders in Benbury in as many weeks.'

'Three?'

'That schoolteacher . . . Moorhouse. I think his name was. Then Mr Franklin. and now this fellow Patterson. He was a solicitor, wasn't he?'

'That's right.'

'Thin, going bald on top?'

'Yes.'

'He was quite pally with Sandy Franklin. He used to come in the shop quite regular. They'd go into a huddle. 'Twas as if he was advising Mr Franklin about something or the other,' she said.

'He was, probably, because he was his solicitor.'

'Yes. I suppose it could have been that.'

'They were both Freemasons, though, and they both attended this lodge,' he added.

'Oh, were they? I didn't know that. And now they're both dead. And that other fellow, Moorhouse. Was he a Mason?'

'I don't know. He might have been. I've never seen him at any meetings though.'

'But he knew Mr Franklin. I remember Mr Franklin saying only last week, when Mr Moorhouse's picture was on the front page of the local paper, that they'd been at school together and—'

'I've got to go!' Bill Smart cut his wife short. 'The police are here. Now don't you worry. I'll be home just as soon as ever I can.'

ELEVEN

If there was one thing which Detective Inspector Ruth Morgan disliked more than anything else it was having to turn out in the middle of the night, especially when it entailed being roused from a deep sleep.

'It's another murder. Stabbed through the back. The man's clothing is in a state of disarray, exactly the same as before,' Detective Sergeant Paddy Hardcastle told her gloomily. 'Would you like me to collect you? Superintendent Wilson's already at the scene.'

'He is?' Ruth swallowed a yawn, suddenly wide awake and fully alert.

'It happened at his Masonic lodge. In the car park.'

She groaned. 'Give me five minutes, and I'll be ready.'

Ruth dressed quickly. It was going to be a long cold night so she might as well be warm, she thought as she pulled on a heavy anorak over her grey slacks and black high-neck sweater. She had a feeling that Superintendent Wilson didn't approve of her anyway, so why worry about what she looked like. He had made it quite clear the last time he had spoken to her that he wasn't very satisfied with the progress she was making in finding whoever had killed John Moorhouse and Sandy Franklin.

The fact that a third murder had taken place, and apparently by the same killer, judging by the state of the victim's clothes, would really put her method of conducting enquiries under question.

She was waiting on the pavement outside her flat when Paddy drew up in a dark-blue unmarked Ford.

'What other information do you have?' she asked as she settled into the passenger seat and fastened her seat belt.

Paddy scowled. 'Not a great deal.'

'You must know something!' Ruth shot him a sideways glance, wondering if he was holding back on her or whether, like her, he was too tired to show enthusiasm.

He shrugged. 'The man's name is Patterson, he's a local solicitor, and he was found just before midnight, by the caretaker, an old boy called Bill Smart.'

'Dead?'

'He was lying across the bonnet of his car with a knife in his back,' he told her laconically.

'And it wasn't the caretaker who killed him?'

'Not very likely since he was the one that called the police.'

'What time did you get there?'

'About twenty minutes before I called you. I expected to find you there, but I was told they hadn't been able to locate you. I only tried your private number on the off chance.'

'I had only been home about fifteen minutes. Just long enough to be in bed and asleep, though.'

'Sorry about waking you, ma'am! A good night out, was it?'

She ignored both the question and the trace of sarcasm. 'You did the right thing,' she said in a tone that she hoped conveyed that the subject was closed.

Detective Superintendent Wilson was very much in evidence when they arrived. He strode across to their car the moment they pulled up, and without any preliminary greeting, barked. 'Are you aware of the details, Inspector?'

'Sergeant Hardcastle has informed me that a Mr Brian Patterson, a local solicitor, was found stabbed—'

'Right here in this car park! I'd been talking to the man only minutes before,' he interrupted. 'We'd both been attending a Masonic meeting. He'd walked across to my car with me, said goodnight, and then went to collect his own car. It must have happened immediately after I'd driven out . . .' His words drifted on to the cold night air, vaporizing into a breathy mist of whiteness as he turned away.

Ruth felt touched by his concern for his friend. Beneath the crusty exterior there was obviously a softer, more human side that he usually kept carefully hidden. If only there was more evidence to go on! More and more it looked like a serial killer at work judging by the state in which the victims were found, and, unless whoever it was had been more careless this time, there was not a single clue to follow up.

Except . . .

She hesitated, then walked over to Detective Superintendent Wilson. 'Excuse me, sir. Both the last two victims were known to each other, and they were both members of your Masonic lodge. Was John Moorhouse also a Mason?'

Inspector Wilson frowned. 'Not to my knowledge. He certainly wasn't in our lodge.' He shot her a piercing look. 'Are you trying to tell me something?'

'No . . . no, not really, sir.'

'Are you suggesting it is some kind of vendetta against Masons?'

She looked startled. 'No. I was only trying to establish a link between the three men. They all appear to be respectable citizens . . . Surely there must be some connection . . .'

'Yes, that they're all dead!' His voice was grim. Accusing, almost.

She wondered if he thought Patterson's death could have been avoided had she been a better detective.

In an uncomfortable silence they walked across the car park to where temporary emergency lighting had been set up and a canvas shelter erected around the scene of the crime.

Ruth was taken aback by the number of officials already there. The scene of crime officer and the forensic medical officer had already carried out their routines and were packing up ready to leave.

'One moment.' Detective Superintendent Wilson laid a restraining hand on the FMO's arm. 'Will you repeat to my inspector what you said earlier about the time of death.'

'As far as I can tell, around eleven o' clock. Might have been a little later. I'll confirm that as soon as I've done the post-mortem.'

Superintendent Wilson looked thoughtful as he turned back to Detective Inspector Morgan and Sergeant Hardcastle. 'He was found by Smart, the caretaker, when he did his final round before locking up for the night.'

'And you say you were with Patterson shortly before eleven p.m., sir?'

'We left the hall together. We'd stayed behind after the others because he had some questions he wanted to ask me.'

'In that case, he must have been killed almost immediately after you parted,' Ruth mused. 'In fact, the killer could have already been in the car park when you drove out.'

'It's possible that Mr Patterson disturbed someone trying to break into his car,' volunteered Sergeant Hardcastle.

Inspector Wilson brushed the suggestion aside. 'Nothing has been taken from the car, and there's no sign of damage.'

'So it must have been someone with a personal grudge against Mr Patterson,' speculated Ruth.

'And do you think this unknown person also had a personal grudge against Franklin and Moorhouse?' snapped Detective Superintendent Wilson.

Once again Ruth was conscious of the implied criticism that this had happened because they had been unable to establish a motive for the two earlier killings, and she bit back the angry reply that hovered on her lips.

It would do no one, least of all herself, any good to antagonize the superintendent. She just wished he would go home and leave her and DS Hardcastle free to pursue their enquiries.

Her silent prayers went unanswered.

An orange glow was already showing on the eastern horizon, heralding a bitterly cold March morning, before Detective Superintendent Wilson finally decided to leave the scene.

'Four o'clock, my office,' he snapped as he headed for his car.

It took a shower, change of clothes, two aspirins, and three cups of strong black coffee before Ruth felt she could face the new day.

She would have preferred to sit down at her desk and study the available evidence to see if there was anything she could deduce from it, but top priority was to accompany DS Hardcastle and interview Mrs Patterson.

She was also anxious to talk to both Tracey Walker and Agnes Walker before facing Detective Superintendent Wilson in his office at four o' clock as he'd ordered.

Skimming through the detailed reports before her, Ruth selected a blank sheet of paper noted down the relevant facts so far obtained.

John Moorhouse, thirty-five. School teacher. Married. Two sons.

Killed in his own home somewhere between five and seven o' clock.

Body found by his wife, Marilyn Moorhouse, when she returned home with their two sons after an evening at Cubs.

They had not been expecting a visitor; there was no sign of forced entry.

Cause of death: multiple stab wounds. Clothing in a state of disarray.

She left a space so that she could note down additional information, should any come to hand, then moved on to record details of the second victim.

Sandy Franklin. Thirty-five. Local newsagent. Bachelor.

Body found in the car park of Accrington Court, a block of luxury flats.

It is believed he was visiting Mrs Tracey Walker, a close friend, at Sixteen Accrington Court.

Cause of death: multiple stab wounds to the back. Clothing in disarray.

A Freemason and member of the same lodge as Detective Superintendent Wilson.

Ruth underlined the last paragraph. It probably wouldn't help them find the killer, but it would remind her of the importance of solving these crimes as speedily as possible, she thought as she moved on to the next victim.

Brian Patterson. Thirty-four. Solicitor. Married. Two daughters.

Body discovered slumped over the bonnet of his car in Masonic car park.

Cause of death: multiple stab wounds. Clothing in disarray

Also a member of the same Masonic lodge as Detective Superintendent Wilson.

Once again, Ruth underscored the last sentence. More and more it seemed like a possible connection. Yet was it? The first victim, Moorhouse, hadn't been a Mason, or if he was he didn't belong to the superintendent's lodge.

The only other things the three men had in common was

that they had all lived in Benbury all their lives and were upright citizens with good reputations.

And they were all about the same age.

She checked the list again. Moorehouse, thirty-four; Franklin, thirty-five; Patterson thirty-five. She wondered if they had been at school together.

The moment Sergeant Paddy Hardcastle came back on duty she queried this with him.

'I can soon check,' he told her.

'I thought perhaps you would know. If they went to the local school they would have been at school with you?'

'I'm thirty-nine. Five years is a big age gap when you're in your teens.'

'The year they started would be the year you left?'

'That's right.' He reached out to pick up the phone. 'It won't take a minute to check it out with the headmaster.'

'No!' She waved the idea away. 'Do that later.' She handed him a sheet. 'These three interviews are more important at the moment.'

There was still a police cordon around the Moorhouse's home at Twenty-Seven Fieldway, and a uniformed constable on duty.

Looking very pale, and fragile, Marilyn Moorhouse answered their questions in almost a monotone.

Her mother had moved in to help look after the two boys. A plump, older version of Marilyn, with a querulous voice and officious manner, she hovered in the background, substantiating her daughter's answers and making it very plain to both Detective Inspector Morgan and Sergeant Hardcastle that she felt it was an intrusion of her daughter's privacy the way the police were asking so many questions.

'One more thing, Mrs Moorhouse. Was your husband a Freemason?'

'He certainly wasn't!' snapped her mother before Marilyn Moorhouse had a chance to do so. 'Nothing but a load of hocus-pocus all that sort of thing if you ask me.'

'Was he at school with either Mr Franklin or Mr Patterson?'

'He was at Benbury Secondary School with Sandy Franklin,' murmured Marilyn. 'Who else did you say?'

'Patterson. Mr Brian Patterson.'

'The solicitor?' Marilyn's blue eyes widened; she looked shocked.

'Yes, that's right.'

'What has he got to do with this?'

'He was killed last night, shortly before midnight . . .'

'Oh no!' The colour drained from her face. 'That's three murders . . .'

'It's absolutely disgraceful! Nothing like this has ever happened in Benbury before,' raged her mother.

'Was Brian Patterson also at school with your husband, Mrs Moorhouse?' persisted Ruth.

'Yes!' Tears cascading down her cheeks, Marilyn Moorhouse nodded. Her blue eyes were dark with fear as she looked up at Ruth. 'Was he . . . was his clothing in the same state as John's?' she breathed hoarsely.

Ruth nodded. 'Yes. I'm afraid so.'

Marilyn Moorhouse shuddered, then buried her face in her hands. 'What does it all mean?' she gulped.

Agnes Walker was a thin, bird-like woman in her late fifties. She could offer them very little help. Although she still lived in the family home, an imposing double-fronted mock-Tudor on the outskirts of Benbury, she hadn't seen Sandy Franklin since her husband had died over five years earlier. Nor did she want to.

'I've heard plenty of gossip about him and that Tracey, mind you,' she told them, 'but as long as my husband took care of the mortgage on this place, and all my household expenses, then he was free to do as he liked as far as I was concerned.

'You weren't divorced?

Agnes Walker bristled like a bantam whose feathers have been ruffled. 'Oh, he asked me for a divorce time and time again, but I'm a Catholic so I had no intention of giving him one.' She laughed, a high, dry sound. 'Now, it doesn't matter. He's dead, the house is mine, and with all the insurance he had I have all the money I need to live comfortable for the rest of my life.'

She sounded so triumphant that it sent a shiver through Ruth.

The idea that Tracey had been two-timing Tom Walker with Sandy Franklin seemed to amuse Agnes. 'Serve him right,' she cackled. 'He led me a dance, going off with that Tracey woman. Calling herself Mrs Walker, I ask you! I'm delighted to know he had a taste of his own medicine. Probably finding out that someone was double-crossing him was what brought on his heart attack.'

She was so vitriolic that Ruth almost wished she could pin Franklin's murder on her. Agnes Walker's alibi ruled that out, however. On the day in question she had been away on a painting holiday in Dorset and had a dozen other participants to prove her whereabouts.

'Well, I think that answers our question as to whether Mrs Walker had any hand in Sandy Franklin's death, don't you?' observed Paddy as they came away from Agnes Walker's home.

'Let's hope we have more success with Tracey Walker.'

'If we are lucky enough to find her at home,' he agreed gloomily.

Tracey was at home, overcome with grief and not prepared to be terribly cooperative. She claimed she had no idea who could have done such a shocking thing. She was quite open about her relationship with the late Tom Walker, and everything she said about it tallied with the information they had on record, or with what Agnes Walker had already told them.

She admitted that Sandy Franklin had been her lover for quite a while before Tom Walker died. She hinted, too, that she had been thinking about moving in with Sandy Franklin.

'I've already given up my lease on this flat,' she said, sniffing. 'In another week or so I'll be homeless.'

Her account of Sandy Franklin's movements on the night he died conformed with information they already had on file. It didn't necessarily eliminate her from suspicion. No one had seen him leave her flat alone. There was always the possibility that she had followed him to where his car was parked, attacked him, and then gone back into her flat.

She'd already heard about Brian Patterson's death, and she confirmed that he and Sandy Franklin had belonged to the same Masonic lodge. 'He was Sandy's solicitor, as well,' she volunteered. 'They'd known each other since their schooldays.'

'Do you mean they went to the same school?'

'That's right. Benbury Secondary School.'

'So did John Moorhouse.'

'Who?' It was obvious that the name meant nothing to Tracey Walker.

'The teacher who was murdered. Did you know him?'

'No, I'd never met him.'

'Do you recall Mr Franklin ever mentioning him?'

Tracey shook her head. Her face was ashen, and her arms wrapped round her body, hugging herself as if in defence against their questioning.

'And no one else was here the evening Mr Franklin came to visit you.'

Again she shook her head.

'And you didn't go to see him off? Watch out of the window so that you could wave goodbye to him when he got in his car or anything like that?'

'Of course not. Why the hell should I get out of a warm bed to wave him goodbye? He could have stayed until morning. I wanted him to,' she added sulkily.

Memories of their parting came flooding back into her mind. She still felt furious with him. Even after she had told him that in less than a week she would be homeless he still hadn't changed his mind about letting her move in with him. He'd seemed to think she was bluffing, even though she'd shown him the lease.

She wondered what the police would think if they knew about the steaming row they'd had before he had stormed out of her flat vowing never to come back again.

That was when he'd told her it was all over between them. They'd ended up shouting obscenities at each other, and when he'd slapped her across the face she'd gone for him, fists flying, determined to wipe the supercilious expression off his face.

TWELVE

The pile of newspapers in Maureen Flynn's living room increased daily. They included the weekly edition of the *Benbury Gazette* as well as every daily newspaper that contained any reference to the Benbury murders.

Hour after hour she sat reading them, comparing the accounts in the popular dailies with the ones in the more serious broadsheets.

The reports varied greatly. The popular papers focused on the more sensational aspects of the murders and speculated wildly on the reasons for them. The broadsheets, for the most part, were coldly factual.

The only items they all agreed on were that the killer had left no fingerprints of any kind or any clues to their identity. They concluded that as the motivation was clearly sexual, it was the work of a dangerous sadist.

Avidly, Maureen studied the potted histories of the victims. She found it fascinating to read the details that each man's family and friends had related to reporters, and to discover the directions their lives had taken since she had left Benbury.

She felt resentful that all of the victims appeared to have had such successful lives. It seemed they had managed to exorcize the event that she had found so traumatic. It had obviously not affected their lives in the way it had blighted hers.

It had now, of course, she thought smugly. Three of them had received their just deserts!

And she'd not finished yet. She was determined to complete her mission . . . and soon. She must do it before the realization of what she had done clouded her mind with guilt.

She felt supercharged. A clarity of mind, and a surge of energy such as she had never known before.

Applying her usual painstaking attention to detail, the same as when she was undertaking any kind of research, she studied every line of the newspaper reports and catalogued the details.

The more she read, the greater was her sense of pride in her achievements. So far there had been no slip-ups whatsoever. Not a single clue, not even a fingerprint left behind! Even the police were baffled.

It was no happy coincidence, she reminded herself. On each occasion she had planned everything with meticulous precision and care. Each time, she had destroyed every vestige of her clothing immediately afterwards. Everything had been put into an unmarked plastic bin bag and taken to a household waste-disposal tip.

She had made sure it was a different tip each time, and that it was over fifty miles away from Benbury and Dutton.

Each complete set of replacements consisting of black track-suit bottoms, trainers, thin rubber gloves, black sweatshirt, and black cagoule had been purchased from shops right away from the area.

Even if she did make a slip-up, and was unfortunate enough to leave some item or the other behind at the scene of the crime, it would be almost impossible to trace who had bought it.

Her work as a researcher had trained her to note the minutest detail, and it was serving her in good stead now. It was a combination of painstaking tabulation plus skill, and an element of good luck, she reflected sagely. She only hoped her luck held out a little while longer. Once it was all over she planned to start a new life.

The first thing she intended to do was move. She'd never liked the poky little place in Dutton. It had been all she could afford when she'd first set up home on her own, but she'd outgrown it a long time ago.

She needed somewhere with plenty of space. A separate room to house her computer and her desk and filing cabinets and the mountain of reference books she needed for her research work. It would be wonderful to have them completely separate so that she would be able to shut the door on that side of her life at the end of the working day.

She dreamed of a spacious sitting room with patio doors leading out on to a terrace and garden. A place where she could relax and entertain friends. Not that she had any friends at the moment, but in the immediate future, when she started out on her new life, she intended to change all that. Everything would be different.

She'd have a cat, too. A long-haired white Persian. Maybe a dog as well. She quite liked the idea of a spaniel. Something big and friendly that she could take for walks.

She'd quite enjoy looking for the right house. Not in Dutton. She'd outgrown that, the same as the place she was living in. It would have to be a town because she needed easy access to a main library and post office. Perhaps she could start by looking in Benbury.

The idea amused her. She rummaged through the pile of newspapers, looking for the *Benbury Gazette*. In the property section, as well as a page of private advertisements, three estate agents each had a full spread.

The name JACKSON caught her eye. As did the passport-sized photograph of the owner heading a short blurb about the excellence of the service he could supply to both vendors and buyers. She ignored the words but concentrated on the face. Lean, handsome with smooth straight black hair parted on the side, exactly the same way as he had worn it at school.

He hadn't changed at all, except that he looked older, more knowing, more arrogant. And, she noted with a smile, he had grown a moustache that helped to hide his thin sneering mouth.

Smiling to herself, Maureen studied the properties Jackson was offering. There was a good mix, but one house in particular, with an address in Englefield Drive, aroused her interest. It was in the more elite area of Benbury, and the picture showed an imposing, detached property with high hedges around a large garden. Central, yet private. Exactly the sort of place she had in mind.

She picked up the phone to make an appointment to see over it the next day. 'I would like it to be Mr Jackson himself who meets me there,' she told the receptionist.

'I don't think Mr Jackson will be free. Our negotiator—'

Maureen cut her short. 'Surely he can manage half an hour sometime during the day. Otherwise I'll leave it.'

'One moment while I check his diary again.'

Maureen crossed her fingers and held her breath, willing Dennis Jackson to meet her there.

'Can you manage four o'clock? It's rather late on in the day, and the best of the light may be gone, but—'

'That will do fine.'

'May I have your name, please?'

Maureen bit down on her lower lip. She hadn't expected that.

'Are you still there?'

'Maitland. Mrs Margaret Maitland.

'Thank you, Mrs Maitland. Now, have you had one of our brochures giving details of the property?'

'No. Perhaps you could ask Mr Jackson to bring one with him.'

'Better still, if you give me your address I'll pop one in the post tonight. If I send it first class you should receive it in the morning.'

'Please don't bother. Mr Jackson can bring it with him,' Maureen said firmly, and put down the phone before the girl could answer.

She felt unnerved by the girl's attitude. She had sounded amused, and she had been so pushy. It was almost as though she was used to women ringing up and making an assignation to meet Dennis Jackson; as though seeing over a property was a standard excuse.

For a moment, Maureen was almost tempted to cancel the appointment.

Maureen Flynn spent the rest of the day anticipating her meeting with Dennis Jackson. For years she'd tried desperately hard to forget him, but now all the suppressed memories came floating to the surface of her mind.

By the time she went to bed that night she felt so overwrought that she was sure she wouldn't sleep. She was tempted to take a sleeping pill, but the fear that it might leave her muddle-headed next day deterred her. Whatever happened, she needed to be one hundred per cent alert if she was to carry through her plan efficiently.

Before she went to bed she laid out ready the clothes she intended to wear next day, checking over every item.

As she had feared, sleep eluded her. She tossed and turned for hours, her mind a seething cauldron of unpleasant memories. When she finally did fall asleep it was into a nightmare world of horror so that she awoke bathed in perspiration and profoundly disturbed.

Fighting back the sour taste in her throat, she showered, hoping the jets of scalding water would cleanse her mind as well as her body.

Over a meagre breakfast of tea and toast she studied the morning papers. There had been no new developments in the Benbury murders so all references to them had been consigned to an inside page both in the tabloids and the broadsheets.

Only the *Mail* had anything new. A profile-interview of Agnes Walker.

The picture the writer painted was of a wife embittered by her husband's philandering. The article spoke of her hate for him, coupled with her animosity towards the woman who had taken the name Walker and had been living with her estranged husband, Tom, at Sixteen Accrington Court. She was far from flattering about Tracey. A flashy blonde strumpet, a money-grabbing whore who'd had her talons into poor Tom, were only a few of the vilifications she used.

Agnes Walker's vindictive condemnation of Sandy Franklin, because he had been associating with Tracey behind Tom Walker's back, was what really amused Maureen. Especially when she read the veiled suggestions Agnes had made concerning Tracey's possible implication in Sandy Franklin's death.

'I'd quite like to meet Agnes Walker, we'd have a lot in common,' she mused aloud as she folded up the *Mail* and placed it with the rest of the pile of newspapers.

She thought about Agnes Walker as she dressed ready to drive to Benbury to meet Dennis Jackson. It would be highly entertaining to have a party, and to invite Agnes Walker, Marilyn Moorhouse, Tracey Walker, and Brian Patterson's wife, and give them a chance to talk things over together.

Maureen frowned. There hadn't been very much in the papers about Sara Patterson, and she wondered why. With or without Mrs Patterson, it would still be a grand wake!

She wondered if they knew each other. Agnes Walker and Sara Patterson had probably met, since their husbands belonged to the same Masonic lodge.

Maureen laughed to herself. Her party would start off as prim and proper as a Masonic Ladies' Night. They'd all be sympathizing with each other over their recent bereavements. A few drinks, though, and if she was any judge of character, Agnes would give vent to her real feelings about her Tom and Tracey. After that the others were bound to join in, and there would be all kinds of revelations.

If they were too reserved to let their hair down then she'd do it for them, Maureen thought vindictively. She'd tell them things about their dear departed that would wipe the tears from their eyes and have them shaking with rage.

By the end of the evening they'd all be secretly relieved that John Moorhouse, Sandy Franklin and Brian Patterson had died when they did.

Dennis Jackson's dark-green Mercedes scrunched to a stop on the gravel driveway outside the Willows in Englefield Drive at ten minutes to four.

Although there wasn't any other car parked in the driveway, he took a quick look round to make sure his prospective client hadn't already arrived, left her car in the roadway and wandered round to the back of the house. Satisfied that he was ahead of her he let himself into the house and made a rapid tour, switching lights on and off, checking taps, flushing toilets, and generally making sure everything was in good working order.

He prided himself on attention to detail, especially when the property was worth over a million. It was a magnificent place: five bedrooms, three reception rooms, a study and a luxuriously fitted kitchen. It was set in half an acre of land-scaped gardens; it was the sort of house he dreamed of owning himself one day.

The previous owner had been born there, and after he married he'd returned to bring up his own family there. He'd died a few months ago at the age of ninety-two, with his children and grandchildren gathered at his bedside. Dennis Jackson considered that was a wonderfully dignified way to end one's life, especially when it was in a setting such as the Willows.

He'd been rather shocked when the family had decided to put the property on the market, but Brian Patterson had told him in confidence that it was on account of death duties.

Satisfied everything was as it should be, he let himself out, locked up, and went back to sit in his car until the prospective buyer arrived. While he waited he studied the details recorded by his receptionist.

It annoyed him that June hadn't insisted on Mrs Maitland giving her address. It told him a great deal if he knew where the client was already living. He could see at a glance whether they were moving up market, or down, and it helped him to judge if it was worth holding out for the asking price or not.

He hoped it wasn't going to be a wild goose chase. If she was merely 'looking the place over' he might well be wasting his time. In his experience, a family home of this magnitude was usually a joint husband and wife decision.

There was always the chance, of course, that she was a wealthy widow and able to make a decision without having to refer to anyone else.

He looked at his gold wrist watch. There was still a minute to go before four o'clock, so he'd give it another five minutes. If she hadn't arrived by then he'd write it off to experience and go back to the office . . . or go home.

He suppressed a shiver. He might as well do that since his mind certainly wasn't on work. No matter how hard he tried he couldn't concentrate.

It was unusual for him to let anything distract him from estate agency matters, but he'd been on edge for several days now. It was all to do with the murders in and around the town. Especially Brian Patterson's!

Looking back, it was almost as if Brian had had some kind of premonition. They'd met by chance, Dennis Jackson recalled, when he'd nipped into the Feathers for a drink on his way home one evening. Brian had been standing at the bar, and right away he'd started talking about the murders.

Dennis had ridiculed Brian's theories as to why John Moorhouse and Sandy Franklin had been murdered. 'You're talking a load of rubbish,' he'd scoffed, incensed that Brian was stirring up memories that he'd tried desperately hard to forget. 'That all happened nearly twenty years ago. We were just kids larking about.'

'There was more to it than that, and you know it!'

'I haven't thought about it for years,' he lied.

'Well, I've thought about it often,' Brian told him. 'I've never been about to put it completely out of my mind. I'll never forget the look on that girl's face.'

'I can't even remember what she looked like!'

'I can still hear her begging us to stop . . . to leave her alone.'

'And are you trying to tell me that you think John Moorhouse, and Sandy Franklin were both murdered because they were there with us that day?'

'I think it's more than likely! I'm positive there's some sort of connection,' Brian insisted, gloomily.

He'd laughed at that. 'More likely a husband of one of Sandy's many girlfriends did him in,' he'd quipped.

'And what about John Moorhouse?' Brian persisted. 'You can hardly say the same about him.'

'I don't know. He might have had a bit on the side.'

'He was a pillar of respectability, and you know it.'

'Well, perhaps his wife had a lover who wanted John out of the way.'

'Now that is utter rubbish!' snapped Brian.

'I don't know why you sound so surprised; most people have secrets of some kind that the people they live with, or associate with, know nothing about,' he'd argued. 'I bet you get to hear a lot of things that would make your hair stand on end. A solicitor is like a doctor, or a priest, in that respect, isn't he?'

Brian had refused to answer, but he'd stayed on the topic of why John Moorhouse and Sandy Franklin had been murdered. 'I'm sure there is a connection between the two murders,' he'd persisted stubbornly.

And even though Dennis had laughed, and told Brian he was paranoid, nevertheless every word Brian had said troubled him. Especially when he read that Brian, too, had been murdered. Stabbed in the back in exactly the same manner as John Moorhouse and Sandy Franklin.

Unable to put Brian's theory out of his mind, he'd rooted through a pile of old photographs when he'd got home, looking for the one that had been taken the day they'd had the results of their A-levels. When he eventually found it he was almost afraid to look at it.

Both John Moorhouse and Sandy Franklin were on it. He was on it as well, and so was Brian Patterson. There was a fifth boy; he couldn't even remember his name now, but he didn't think he was around Benbury any longer.

The rest of them had all become men of some importance in the town. John Moorhouse had been deputy headmaster at Benbury Secondary School, Sandy Franklin had owned a thriving newsagent's, and Brian Patterson had been one of the town's leading solicitors.

He'd stared at the picture mesmerized. And he owned the largest estate agency in Benbury.

There was also a girl in the photograph. Thin, dark hair and nondescript, she'd been the studious type; quiet as a mouse. They'd insisted that she went with them when they'd gone off to celebrate. After all, it was quite an achievement for a girl to have done as well as them in the exams.

Celebrate! Dennis Jackson suddenly felt cold inside at the memory.

It wasn't only the fact that they'd all got blind drunk, or that they had spiked the girl's drinks so that she, too, was legless, it was what happened afterwards.

That was what tormented him. And he'd been the instigator!

The others had probably been able to put it out of their minds afterwards. He never had. He'd been haunted ever since by the terrible things he'd done to the girl, and what he'd egged the others on to do.

He struggled to push the memory from his mind as he heard the scrunch of wheels on the gravel, and a red Ford Escort came to a stop a few yards behind his own car.

In his rear mirror he watched as a trim, dark-haired woman of about thirty stepped out on to the drive. She was wearing a dark-grey suit with a white blouse, dark tights, and sensible low-heel court shoes.

His immediate gut reaction was that he was about to waste the next half hour. If he was any judge, this woman was about as likely to purchase the Willows as he was to buy Buckingham Palace. By the look of her car, and the way she was dressed, she wouldn't even be able to afford the council tax, let alone the house.

Not unless she's come up on the Pools, or won on the Lottery, he told himself as he locked his car and strode across the gravel to meet her, an ingratiating smile of welcome on his face.

THIRTEEN

The atmosphere in the incident room at Benbury police station was unbearably tense as Detective Superintendent James Wilson cross-questioned DI Morgan, and DS Hardcastle about the three murders. His manner was both disgruntled and overbearing; it was almost as if they were undergoing a third-degree.

Reluctantly, Ruth admitted that so far they had had very little success in tracking down the killer or killers.

Even Paddy, the seasoned detective, was puzzled and disheartened by the lack of evidence. 'I'm beginning to wonder if it's the work of a contract killer. Each murder has the same hallmark, especially this sadomasochistic tendency of leaving the victim's clothes in a state of disarray.'

'Someone so highly experienced that they know exactly how to cover their tracks,' mused Superintendent Wilson.

'Precisely, sir. So far we've virtually drawn a blank even though we've interviewed each of the families and their neighbours. In the case of Sandy Franklin, we've even interviewed his staff, and most of his regular customers.'

'And what about information from Forensic?' barked Superintendent Wilson.

'They've only been able to say that in each case death resulted from repeated stabbings with a knife.'

'No other clues at all?' His voice indicated that he was far from satisfied with the answer.

'Not really, sir,' Ruth affirmed. 'Nothing substantial. Except . . .' She hesitated. 'Except one very indistinct footprint at the scene of the third murder.'

'Traceable?'

'Possibly, sir. We're still investigating. So far we know it is a trainer type of shoe, and that where the instep has made contact with the ground there appears to be the imprint of a logo of some kind.'

'Nothing else?'

'I haven't, but . . .' Ruth paused and looked across at Paddy, signalling him, with a lift of her eyebrows, to continue.

He probably thought the red car was too trifling a matter to mention, but since they were so short of any real evidence at least it would prove that they were leaving no stone unturned in their effort to track down the killer.

'When we were doing house-to-house enquiries two people mentioned seeing a red Ford parked a few yards from John Moorhouse's house on the night he was murdered,' Paddy stated.

'Humph.' Wilson shot them both a glance from under his hooded lids. 'That's not much to go on, is it!'

'Fieldway is a cul-de-sac, and most of the neighbours not only know each other's cars, but also recognize those belonging to regular visitors.'

So did you get its number?'

'Afraid not, sir. No one thought to note it down.'

Irritated, Detective Superintendent Wilson drummed with his fingers on the table in front of him.

'It might be worth another try,' Ruth murmured in an attempt to appease him.

'Yes. Do that! People can sometimes recall numbers or letters, even though at the time they think they hadn't noticed them,' he agreed shrewdly. He stood up, his massive bulk towering over her. 'And make sure you have this shoe imprint checked out, Inspector. You'd better make it top priority since it seems to be the only piece of evidence we have.'

Questioning the residents in the Fieldway proved to be completely abortive. One of the women who had reported seeing the red Ford Escort now wasn't even sure if it had been that make of car, only that it had been a red one. She'd only been aware of it at all because it had been parked so close to the entrance to her driveway that it had made turning in rather difficult.

When they knocked on the Moorhouse's door there was no answer. A neighbour informed them that Mrs Moorhouse and the two boys had gone to stay with her mother.

'She couldn't stand being in the house after what happened,' the woman commented. 'She said every time she went into the sitting room she imagined she could see poor John lying on the floor there.'

'We wanted to ask her about a red Ford Escort that was parked near here the night her husband was murdered,' Ruth explained. 'Did you see it, by any chance?'

The woman shook her head and made it quite plain that she didn't wish to be questioned any further. She stepped back into her hallway, closing the door quickly, almost in their faces.

'So what's next?' demanded Ruth as they walked back to their car.

'We could go along to Accrington Court and have another word with Tracey Walker,' Paddy suggested.

Once again they drew a blank. The caretaker informed them that she'd vacated the flat the previous day, and that she had not left any forwarding address.

'That makes her one notch higher on our list of suspects,' commented Paddy.

'She did tell us that the lease was up, and that she would have to leave the flat quite soon,' Ruth reminded him.

'She should have told us where we could contact her, though.'

'Maybe she will in a day or so, when she has settled in at her new address. In the meantime perhaps we should talk to Mrs Patterson.'

Sara Patterson was in her early thirties and slim, with clean-cut features, vivid blue eyes, and dark hair sculpted to her head. She was dressed in dark-blue jeans and a stylish blue and white striped shirt. Quite composed, despite her recent ordeal, she invited them into her sunny lounge and insisted on making them all coffee before she sat down to answer their questions.

She'd been married to Brian for twelve years, she told them, and they had two daughters. Alice was ten, and Jane was almost eight. They both attended Benbury Junior School. She could throw no light on why Brian had been killed.

'He was very late leaving the Masonic hall on the night in question,' murmured Ruth.

'Almost the last, according to the caretaker,' confirmed Paddy. 'Weren't you worried when he was so late coming home?'

'I wasn't here.'

Ruth and Paddy both looked surprised.

Sara Patterson's colour rose but she offered no explanation for her absence from home.

'So Mr Patterson was in no hurry to get home because he knew you were out?' Paddy said thoughtfully.

'He intended to stay on after the meeting to talk to your superintendent. I thought you would have known that,' she answered pertly.

'We do have that information, but we don't know why he wanted to talk to Superintendent Wilson. Do you?'

'Brian was to have become master at the next meeting,' she said diffidently. 'James Wilson is the present master, and there were several things Brian wanted to know, so after the main meeting was over seemed to be a good time to talk to him. Brian is . . .' She paused and bit down on her lower lip. 'Brian *was* a stickler for details, and very anxious to do everything properly when he was installed, you see.'

'But you were away from home, Mrs Patterson,' persisted Ruth.

'Yes!' As if conscious that her tone had been abrupt to the point of rudeness she repeated her affirmation in a more moderated voice. 'Yes, I was away.'

'And your children?'

'They were staying overnight with my mother.'

'So your husband knew there would be no one at home when he returned.'

'Yes. Of course he did. He didn't expect his meeting to end until quite late . . .'

'Does this mean you weren't returning home until sometime the following morning?'

'Morning . . . early afternoon . . . I hadn't made any firm plans except to be home in time to pick the two girls up from school,' she said with some asperity.

'Where did you say you were staying, Mrs Patterson?'

'I didn't.'

'I'm afraid we will have to know.'

Sara Patterson looked annoyed. For a moment Ruth thought she was going to refuse to answer.

'If you must know, I was visiting my sister,' she snapped.

'In Benbury?'

'No, of course not! She lives in London.'

'And was this a social visit?'

'A shopping trip actually. I needed something special to wear at Brian's Ladies' Night.'

'That won't be for quite some time, will it?' Paddy frowned. Although not a Freemason himself he knew enough about the ritual to know she wouldn't be attending her husband's inauguration.

'I thought it would be one less thing for him to worry about if he knew I had the right dress.'

'So it was a shopping spree to London?'

'Yes.' Her reply was terse, and she seemed nervous.

'Would you let us have your sister's address and telephone number, Mrs Patterson . . . so that we can check out the information you have given us,' murmured Ruth.

Sara's blue eyes widened in astonishment. 'You mean you don't believe me?'

'It's not a question of believing or disbelieving. In a case of this kind we have to double check every detail.'

Aware that Sara Patterson could hardly contain her anger, Ruth switched the line of enquiry. 'Going back to your husband, Mrs Patterson,' she said smoothly, 'do you know if he had any enemies?'

Still looking hostile, Sara Patterson shrugged. 'Not as far as I am aware. As a solicitor he dealt with the affairs of a wide range of people, so I suppose there could have been someone who might have had a grudge against him.'

'Do you mean one of his clients?'

She frowned. 'It could have been someone he'd defended in court, and they'd lost their case . . .' Her voice trailed away uncertainly. She shrugged and spread her hands. 'I really don't know. I'm just hazarding a guess.'

'Was your husband a friend of either of the other two men who have been killed in Benbury?'

Some of the colour drained from Sara Patterson's face. 'Not really. He knew them both. Sandy Franklin was in the same Masonic lodge. Surely, you must know that since Superintendent Wilson is the master of their lodge,' she added caustically.

'And John Moorhouse?'

She shrugged. 'He was at school with Brian. We hardly ever saw him or Marilyn though. John wasn't in the Masons, or in the same social circle as us.'

'Why was that?' Ruth looked at Sara Patterson enquiringly, encouraging her to explain more fully.

'The Moorhouses were into amateur dramatics, and parent/ teacher fund-raising events, that sort of thing. Marilyn was tied up with the Cubs, and all sorts of charities. Do-gooders, I suppose you'd say they were!'

'Not your scene?'

'I support various charities, and Brian gave a great deal of his time, and money, to Masonic charitable concerns,' she retorted sharply.

'On a slightly different level, though.'

She shrugged again. 'Yes, you could say that. Brian also belonged to the Benbury Golf Club, and we had quite a busy social life.'

'And John Moorhouse didn't play golf?'

She shook her head. 'If he did, he didn't belong to the Benbury Club. Mind you, it's not all that easy to become a member. Sandy Franklin has been trying for years . . . I don't suppose it matters now,' she ended abruptly.

'Did you and your husband see very much of Sandy Franklin?'

Sara Patterson's face tightened. 'Only at Masonic events. Brian avoided him socially.'

'Really! Why was that?'

Sara Patterson looked uncomfortable. 'I'm not sure.'

'I've heard he was something of a ladies' man,' commented Paddy. 'Would you say there was any truth in that, Mrs Patterson?'

Sara Patterson bit down on her lower lip but didn't answer.

'Did your husband prefer that you shouldn't be in Sandy Franklin's company because he was afraid Mr Franklin might be tempted to make a pass at you and—'

'What utter rubbish! How dare you make such an accusation.' Sara Patterson's face was livid, and her vivid blue eyes flashed angrily.

'Please, Mrs Patterson,' Ruth intervened quickly, 'Sergeant Hardcastle was only trying to establish if there was any foundation for the rumours about the sort of man Mr Franklin was.'

Although Sara Patterson remained silent she appeared to be uneasy, despite the inspector's intervention, and avoided their eyes.

'Is there anything further you can tell us that might help us with our enquiries?'

'No. Nothing at all.'

'Any other link between Moorhouse, Franklin, and your husband, other than he was the same age as them, and that he also went to Benbury Secondary School?' persisted Ruth.

Sara Patterson looked at her watch. 'I've told you all I know, and now, if you'll excuse me, I have to collect my girls from school.'

Purposefully, she walked through into the hall, selected a jacket from the hall stand, and picked up her keys, leaving Ruth and Paddy no alternative but to follow her.

Her car was on the driveway. As she unlocked it, Paddy solicitously held the door, waiting until she slid behind the wheel before closing it.

Sara Patterson felt uneasy as she drove her red Astra towards Benbury Junior School to collect Alice and Jane. She wished she hadn't told the two detectives that she had been at her sister's. She should have said London and left it at that.

When they'd insisted on knowing where she'd stayed overnight she could have named a hotel, not given them Yvonne's address and phone number. That had been a stupid thing to do, and if they did phone to check on whether she had stayed the night there Yvonne certainly wouldn't be very pleased at being involved.

If she'd given them a false address, though, that would have looked even worse if they'd checked it out and then found she'd been lying.

As she sat outside the school waiting for the children to

come out she went over in her mind all the things she had
told DI Morgan and DS Hardcastle.

And the things she hadn't.

Trust Brian not to be around when she needed him. He
would have known what to say. That was if she could have
brought herself to tell him.

It was like some dreadful nightmare, she thought apprehen-
sively. She really ought to make a note of what she'd said to
the police. It wouldn't look good if they questioned her again,
and she changed her story. And somehow she thought they
might.

The detective sergeant had looked at her as if he thought
that she might have been the one who killed Brian. And if he
ever found out that she hadn't stayed the night at Yvonne's,
he might start digging deeper.

Anxiously, she rummaged in the glove pocket of the car for
a biro and some paper to write on.

She couldn't find a pen, but there was a stub of yellow
pencil belonging to one of the girls and a discarded supermarket
bill. That would have to do, she decided. She'd write on the
back of it. With so much on her mind at the moment she
couldn't afford to trust to her memory.

FOURTEEN

The car belonging to DI Morgan and DS Hardcastle was parked in the roadway outside the Patterson's house, and they were still sitting there discussing the outcome of their interview with Sara Patterson when she drove out of her driveway.

'She has a red car,' observed Paddy as the red Astra sped past them. He handed the inspector a small crumpled piece of paper. 'This parking ticket is from the Meadway car park, which is the public car park right alongside the Masonic hall. The date is smudged, but it should still be possible to verify if her car was parked there the night her husband was murdered.'

Ruth frowned as she smoothed out the fragment of evidence. 'You removed this from her windscreen. Does this mean you think Sara Patterson may have murdered her husband,' she said, in a surprised voice.

It was a statement rather than a question, and Paddy grinned. 'I was trained to believe that everyone is a suspect until proved otherwise, ma'am,' he replied blandly.

'Even if she did kill her husband, she could hardly be held responsible for the other two murders!'

'No, perhaps not,' he conceded. 'We won't know that for certain until we've checked upon her movements. I don't think she was telling the truth about her visit to London.'

'She was rather evasive, I quite agree.'

'And if she isn't in any way connected with the other two murders then this could have been a copycat murder. What better way than to use the procedure established by some other killer so that they would also be suspected of the murder you have committed.'

Ruth looked at him mockingly. 'Your theory sounds far too convoluted to be the work of Sara Patterson. She's petty, and snobbish, but I hardly think she has that sort of cunning. Anyway, we have no evidence.'

'A red car was seen outside John Moorhouse's place the night he was killed.'

'That was a Ford Escort.'

'Was it? The woman who reported it couldn't be sure what make of car it was, only that it was red.'

'Sara Patterson said her husband rarely saw anything of John Moorhouse . . .'

'She didn't mention whether *she* ever saw him or not.'

'Are you suggesting that not only did Sara Patterson murder her own husband, but she was also having an affair with John Moorhouse, and possibly murdered him as well?'

Paddy shook his head. 'I don't know. It's a possibility worth considering. She had every opportunity. And she doesn't seem to be overly distressed by her husband's demise.'

'She might be trying to bear up because of the children,' Ruth told him tartly. 'Or it might be delayed shock.'

'I don't think she told us the entire truth about her trip to London,' he repeated stubbornly.

'She gave us her sister's name and phone number . . . We can always check.'

Paddy shook his head. 'Her sister will vouch she was there. I'm quite sure about that. She's probably provided an alibi countless times before.'

'You mean Sara Patterson regularly goes to London for something other than to see her sister or go shopping?'

'Yes! That is if she even goes to London. It's more than likely that she simply uses her sister as an alibi.'

'In case her husband should try to contact her for some reason?'

'Right!' He gave a dry laugh.

'So who looks after the children overnight?'

'On this occasion, her husband was out at a Masonic meeting, so it was her mother,' he reasoned.

'Yes. She did tell us that,' agreed Ruth thoughtfully.

'Leaving that point in abeyance for the moment,' Paddy went on, 'did you notice any change in her manner when we spoke about Sandy Franklin?'

Ruth frowned. 'She appeared to colour up, and she looked embarrassed. Rather reluctant to talk about him, in fact.'

'Exactly!' Paddy sounded triumphant. 'It's my conjecture that at some time or other Sara Patterson has been involved with Sandy Franklin. Had an affair with him!'

'But surely—'

'Believe me, I've been working this patch for a long time. I started as a constable in Benbury, and that was almost twenty years ago. The affairs Sandy Franklin has had in that length of time have been legion. He put a girl in the family way even before he left school.'

'You really think that Sara Patterson would become involved with a man like that?'

He shrugged. 'You never can tell. She's very attractive; you could hardly say the same for Patterson.'

Ruth frowned. 'Even so, as a solicitor he has a reputation to uphold, and he'd hardly tolerate his wife becoming involved with one of his clients.'

'I wasn't suggesting she still was involved, and she certainly couldn't have been seeing him the night her husband was murdered, not unless she was visiting him in the morgue.'

'Precisely! Sandy Franklin was already dead, so is there any point in discussing it? We'll need something far more concrete than conjectures of that sort if we are going to keep Superintendent Wilson happy,' Ruth pointed out a trifle sharply.

'You have to admit, though, that she was certainly very uneasy when Sandy Franklin's name was mentioned,' insisted Paddy.

'Maybe it was the blunt manner in which you broached the subject,' Ruth told him caustically. 'I would have used a more subtle approach.'

Paddy looked annoyed. His mouth tightened, and his square chin jutted angrily. 'What line of enquiry do you wish to proceed with next, ma'am?' he asked in a clipped tone.

'I think we should get back to the station and phone Yvonne Duran, and see if she can tell us anything useful about her sister's shopping trip to London, don't you?'

The journey was made in strained silence.

Although she welcomed the opportunity to follow her own line of reasoning without interruption, Ruth was sorry she had upset Paddy.

He probably does know far more about the local people than I do, she reflected. Nevertheless, their enquiries must be done according to the book, not as the result of mere intuition, or the personal quirks of local personalities.

It would be all too simple to let Paddy influence her judgement with hearsay and speculation. And she had no doubt that Superintendent Wilson would take a vindictive delight in pointing out the error of her suppositions if she concocted a case on such superficial evidence.

This was not an easy investigation, but she was determined to find the murderer, or murderers, and prove to both Paddy Hardcastle and James Wilson that appointing a woman as the CID Inspector had not been a retrograde step for the Benbury police. She suspected that, although he tried not to show it, Paddy resented both her appointment and her methods of investigation. He probably found it hard to accept that techniques had changed, and that his pedantic methods not only lacked finesse, but that they'd been superseded by a sharper, more scientific mode.

It was understandable. He'd been in the Benbury police for almost twenty years, and had risen from the ranks, and not had the benefit of transferring to Police Training College straight from university. Doubtless, however, he must have anticipated that after all his years of valuable service, and his satisfactory work as a detective, he'd be the next CID Inspector.

She shot a surreptitious sideways glance at him. His anger showed in every fibre of his bearing. From the way he gripped the steering wheel, so that his knuckles shone like white ivory, to the set of his jaw.

She studied him covertly. His anger, far from detracting from his good looks, seemed to enhance them, she reflected with grim amusement. As well as exceptionally broad shoulders, he had the muscular physique of a man who spent a great deal of time keeping fit. His thick fair hair, brushed back from his deep forehead, framed clean-shaven cheeks that gleamed with health; the only blemish was a faint scar to one side of his square jaw. When he smiled, his amiable grin showed a row of strong white teeth.

In fact, she decided, he really was extremely handsome, and

she wondered why he had never married. True, as he had explained, being in the police did give rise to unsociable hours. Even so, a lot of women would have overlooked that in exchange for the comfort of having someone so solid and dependable.

Perhaps that was his problem. He was too solid, too set in his ways. Not yet forty, yet his manner was as cautious as if he was in his late-fifties. In his usual garb of tweed jacket, and buff-coloured cords, he looked more like a farmer, or a country squire, than a policeman.

His social life seemed to consist of going to the local for a pint and listening to gossip. She was surprised that he paid any attention to tittle-tattle, but she supposed it was inevitable if he went to the pub every night. And he probably did that because he was lonely, she thought compassionately.

She felt guilty because she had consistently rebuffed his attempts at friendship. As a woman doing what was generally regarded as a man's job she had thought it was the most sensible way to handle the situation. Perhaps she had been a little too restrained. When they got back to the station she'd suggest going for a coffee together. She hated going into the police canteen – it was so basic with its Formica topped tables, and metal chairs – but if it helped to soften up the tension between them then it would be a small sacrifice to make.

Her good intentions were undermined the moment they entered the building.

'Detective Superintendent Wilson requested that you should both report to his office the moment you came in,' the desk sergeant informed them.

'Trouble?' Paddy's dark brows lifted almost imperceptibly as he held the door from reception to the rear offices open for her.

'It certainly sounds ominous.'

Superintendent Wilson's voice as he greeted them left them in no doubt that there had been a further development.

'I've been trying to reach you for well over an hour,' he barked. 'Don't you keep your intercom switched on, Sergeant?'

'We've only been in the car for the past ten minutes, sir. Before that we were at Nineteen The Crescent.'

'Interviewing Mrs Sara Patterson,' Ruth told him.

From under hooded brows, Superintendent Wilson looked from her to Sergeant Hardcastle and then back again. 'And the result of your interview?'

It was obvious he was expecting them to relate some outstanding news. When neither of them spoke, he placed his elbows on the desk, and supporting his chin on his finger tips, stared directly at them.

'Surely you have something to report, Inspector?'

Ruth shook her head. 'Not a great deal, I'm afraid, sir. Mrs Patterson wasn't at home the night her husband was murdered. She was in London on a shopping spree.'

'She can confirm this?'

'She claims to have been staying with her sister, Yvonne Duran. We have a telephone number and—'

'And have you checked it out? Has the sister confirmed her story?'

'We haven't made contact yet, sir. We would have done it the moment we got back, only the desk sergeant informed us that—'

Superintendent Wilson waved her explanation away. 'Any other information?' he barked.

Ruth looked expectantly at Paddy. 'The sergeant has a car parking ticket . . .'

'Taken from Mrs Patterson's car, sir. It's one from the machine in the public car park near the Masonic hall.'

Superintendent Wilson looked puzzled. 'Do you mean for the night her husband was murdered?'

'I don't know about that, sir. The date and time are both smudged—'

'But we will be able to verify when it was issued from the serial number,' Ruth interrupted.

'And Mrs Patterson does have a red car, sir.'

Superintendent Wilson frowned. 'Red car?'

'A red car was seen parked in Fieldway the night John Moorhouse was murdered,' Ruth reminded him.

The superintendent's face froze. 'Are you telling me that you think that Mrs Patterson murdered Moorhouse, and then her husband? Perhaps we should include Sandy Franklin as well for good measure,' he added sarcastically when they both remained silent.

Ruth sensed that Paddy had a cynical smile on his face as he looked conspiratorially at the superintendent. In her eagerness to appease Superintendent Wilson, and to show that they were doing everything possible to catalogue the movements of everyone connected with the murders, she'd made a glaring mistake. By stating what was little more than a supposition she'd undermined her own authority.

She wondered if Paddy had set her up deliberately, hinting that perhaps Sara Patterson had been in some way involved, and then leaving her to blurt it out. Was there a sharp, devious mind behind that bluff exterior?

In that moment she hated both him and Inspector Wilson. It was as if they were both conspiring against her. If Sergeant Hardcastle had been the one to make such a statement, Superintendent Wilson would have regarded it as valuable evidence, she thought resentfully.

Well, they might think it was a man's world, and that as a woman she wasn't up to the job, but she was determined to prove them wrong. 'If you'll excuse me, sir, she said stiffly, 'I'll go and telephone Yvonne Duran, and see if she can confirm Mrs Patterson's movements the night her husband was murdered.'

'By all means!' He frowned heavily. 'I appreciate that this is a very difficult case, Inspector, but it would set a great many minds at rest if you could come up with even one single fragment of watertight evidence.'

FIFTEEN

June Lowe studied the red fingernails on her left hand, then shrugged her slim, shapely shoulders as she replaced the receiver she had been holding to her right ear for several minutes.

If Mrs Jackson was out, and hadn't left the answerphone switched on, then there wasn't a lot she could do to about passing on the message Dennis Jackson had asked her to deliver before he'd gone to Englefield Drive to show a client over the Willows.

She looked at her silver and blue enamel watch. It was a few minutes to six. She didn't know what to do for the best. She'd had no luck contacting him either, and he'd asked her to remind him that he must leave early as he and his wife were going to a rather special dinner party.

Well, she'd done her best, she told herself as she picked up her handbag and her car keys.

Her hand on the door, June hesitated. Perhaps she ought to try once more. He must surely have finished showing Mrs Margaret Maitland around the Willows by now. If he was on his way home she might be able to get him on his mobile and then she could explain she'd not been able to contact his wife.

When she still had no success, June felt concerned. His wife would kill him if he was late. By the sound of it their dinner date was quite an important affair so he'd have to change into evening clothes.

Earlier on she'd thought he'd simply switched off his phone so as not to be distracted while he was dealing with the client. The appointment at the Willows had been for four o' clock. He couldn't still be there.

The only other thing she could think was that perhaps he'd taken the client for a coffee. She'd sounded quite young so maybe he was putting on his charm act in the hope of clinching the deal. Or, perhaps she was just attractive, June mused. It wouldn't be the first time that he'd fallen for a pretty face and found something better to do than return to the office. She hated it when that happened because she always felt such a fool when she had to cover up for him.

June was pretty certain that Deborah Jackson wasn't taken in by her explanations even though she never openly queried them. This time, she reflected, she'd done her best, and he'd have to make his own excuses if he was late getting home.

She switched off the lights and keyed in the code that activated the burglar alarm. It wasn't her problem, she told herself as she pulled the door shut behind her, but it worried her all the same. She was his personal assistant, though, not his keeper, she reminded herself as she unlocked the door of her red Mini. She had her own life to lead, and it didn't include worrying about her boss – leastways, not when her working day was over.

June sighed. That was one of her failings; she was too conscientious, especially where Dennis Jackson was concerned. She sighed again. It was the sort of effect he seemed to have on most women from eighteen to eighty. A dynamic personal charm that was irresistible.

To set her mind at rest, June decided to drive home by way of Englefield Drive and see if Dennis Jackson's car was still there. But what if it was? What did she do then? she asked herself. Ring on the doorbell? And if he didn't answer should she shout, 'Your wife is expecting you home!' through the letter box?

The thought amused her. It would serve him right if she did do that, she thought rebelliously, especially if he was still in the house with the client, Margaret Maitland.

She sighed. If Dennis Jackson wasn't so good looking, and so charismatic, would she be doing all this? The truth was, she felt so flattered when he treated her as a confidante that she found herself anxious to protect him. Besides, he was always so grateful whenever she covered up for him. Absolutely charming. And the next day he always brought her flowers, or chocolates, or perfume, in appreciation of what she had done. He never forgot her birthday, either. Flowers, as well as a card and a present. And he always gave her something really gorgeous at Christmas, as well as a bonus in her wage packet.

He'd never made a pass at her, but she sometimes wondered if deep down he fancied her. She noticed the way his dark eyes lit up whenever she was wearing something that was particularly sexy. And when she wore a mini he couldn't keep his eyes off her legs!

Probably the only reason he didn't make a pass at her was because he valued her too much. She could run the office single-handed, and often did when he was on one of his sprees. Perhaps if she hadn't been quite so efficient there'd be a different kind of rapport between them.

June gave rein to her fantasies as she drove towards Englefield Drive. She didn't fancy being his mistress – that was too risky, and you only got yourself talked about. Married and enjoying the glamorous lifestyle that went with being Mrs Jackson was more her style. A big house, someone to clean it, parties every week, a swimming pool, and luxury holidays abroad, that was her ambition.

Supposing his car was still outside The Willows, and he was there on his own? If she went in and there was just the two of them there then absolutely anything could happen! Even thinking about it she experienced a bizarre excitement.

Taking one hand from the steering wheel, she fluffed out her blonde hair, and then undid the top two buttons of her blouse so that the neck was open in a seductive manner.

'It could be fun,' she told herself aloud. In fact, a damn sight more fun than anything that ever happened between her and Duncan White, who was her current boyfriend.

June let her fantasy build up. She pictured herself telling Dennis Jackson how she felt about him, how the way he flirted, and carried on with all the women clients, excited her. She would even tell him that covering up for him when his wife phoned, asking if she knew where he was, turned her on.

If she had to choose between Dennis Jackson and Duncan White then Dennis would win hands down. He had the looks, the charm, and – something which, in her eyes, was even more important – he had experience. The tales she'd heard about him since she'd been working at the estate agency were legion.

She was pretty sure they were true because of the number of women who came into the office to see him. And not all of them wanted to buy houses, either.

Yes, she decided, if his was the only car outside the Willows then she'd take it as an omen and chance her arm.

As she turned into the gravel drive she was almost afraid to look. And when she did, her heart thundered crazily. It was an omen all right!

'Now or never,' she told herself aloud as she parked her red Mini behind Jackson's dark-green Mercedes, 'Now or never,' she repeated as she marched purposefully towards the house.

She stopped in surprise, her hand poised to ring the bell. The door was already ajar.

Deborah Jackson surveyed herself in the ornate pier glass on the wall between the oyster velvet curtains that framed the two tall windows in the elegant master bedroom at High Winds.

She had spent an awful lot of money on the little black velvet number she was wearing, but it had been an investment: the result was terrific.

Slowly, she twisted around, craning her neck so that she could study the effect from every angle. She hoped Dennis would be impressed, since he would be paying for it.

She raised both arms and lifted her shoulder-length hair, then let it fall slowly, like a fiery curtain as it swept down on to her creamy shoulders.

Yes, he'd be paying for it. And not just for the dress. Tonight would be the ultimate test of whether she decided to let things remain as they were, or whether she divorced him.

She picked up a lipstick from her rosewood dressing table, and added another scarlet layer to her wide mouth.

He must know that she was aware that he was carrying on with Martina Carpenter. If he didn't then he'd be in no doubt about it before the evening was over.

His face had been almost too impassive when she'd told him they were dining with the Carpenters, and she'd detected a note of unease in his voice that showed he'd been taken aback.

'I thought you didn't like the Carpenters!'

'I don't.'

'Then why are we dining with them?'

'You keep telling me what important clients they are, and you spend so much time trying to find exactly the right sort of property to meet Martina's requirements, that I thought it was time I showed an interest in them.'

'You mean we're entertaining them?'

'That's right. At Alfonso's.'

His brows had shot up. It was the most expensive restaurant in the Benbury area.

'So make sure you're home early. In plenty of time to change. I've had your dinner jacket cleaned, and I've bought you a wonderful new shirt.'

'Why all the fuss? They've already agreed to buy Wetherby House, didn't I tell you?'

'No!' She smiled sweetly. 'Well, we can make it a celebration, and since they've been such special clients it will be a wonderful way of saying thank you for their business, won't it?'

He'd been about to argue, but she could see he was unsure of himself. He didn't know quite how much *she* knew about his latest affair.

Tonight, Deborah decided, would bring matters to a head. Tonight he might have to choose between her and Martina Carpenter.

In the past she had ignored his countless romantic liaisons. She'd known the sort of man he was when she'd married him. Anything in a skirt could turn his head. But his affairs were never serious. A fling lasted a few days, or at the most a couple of weeks, and then it was all over . . . until the next time.

She'd learned to profit from his adventures. Rewards had included a gold brooch; a jewelled watch; an emerald ring; countless holidays; even a stunning red sports car.

Only, this time it seemed to be so much more serious. The few weeks had become a few months. This time his flirtation showed no signs of ending. Which was why she had decided it was time for action. Unless he gave up Martina, the dumpy little Spanish bimbo, then she wanted a divorce and a settlement that would make his eyes water.

She pirouetted once again, feeling confident, knowing that she looked good. The smooth black velvet enhanced her tall, curvaceous figure. Beside her, Martina would look not only dumpy, but frumpish in her fussy, frilly frock. And her long red-gold hair, skimming her creamy shoulders, framing her finely chiselled features, would contrast sharply with Martina's sallow complexion and the straight black hair that she wore in a severe chignon.

Deborah didn't really mind which way things went. In some ways it would be a relief to be free of Dennis and his insatiable sexual demands. At thirty-two she was still young enough to resume the acting career she'd given up when they'd married. It would be wonderful to get right away from Benbury, too. She felt trapped in the monotonous round of dinner parties that seemed to be all the town offered in the way of social entertainment.

Wherever they went, whether it was to the golf club, Ladies' Night at the Masonic hall, the Conservative Club, or simply to one of the local night clubs, it was always the same faces. She knew absolutely everything there was to know about the group they mixed with, and she despised them all. The women, because at one time or another they'd all succumbed to Dennis's charms and either flirted with him or had an affair with him. She despised the men because they continued to treat him as a friend even though most of them suspected they'd been cuckolded by him.

Over the years she'd watched Dennis flirt with all their wives. And when he'd tired of them she'd seen the expression in their eyes change from 'come-hither' to hate. She'd over-heard cloakroom confidences between those who'd fallen for his charms, and been disillusioned, or heart-broken, by his eventual rejection.

With or without Dennis she intended to change her lifestyle. London was her Mecca. Not just for the shops, but for the theatres and restaurants, and the variety of social opportunities to be found if you moved in the right circles. And that was what she intended to do – and without Dennis. In the past she'd stood passively by while he had his fling. Now it was her turn.

She looked at her jewelled watch, the latest of his gifts to mollify her, and frowned. It was much later than she had thought. If they didn't leave soon they'd be late. Surely he hadn't forgotten about their dinner date after she'd reminded him to be home early? Perhaps she should check if he was still at the office, although she didn't think that was very likely since she had made a point of phoning June Lowe earlier in the day and asking her to make sure he left on time. And June never, ever let her down.

Deborah Jackson was halfway down the stairs when the phone rang.

SIXTEEN

D ennis Jackson was still as tall and good-looking as she'd remembered, Maureen Flynn thought as she watched him walk across to meet her. Maturity suited him. He had filled out, his shoulders had broadened, and it had given him an added confidence that showed in his stride and the way he carried himself.

Laughing to herself, she slung her cumbersome brown holdall bag over one shoulder, trying not to let herself appear weighed down by it, and walked across the gravel to meet him.

'Mrs Maitland? How very pleasant to meet you!'

His smile was so warm, his handshake so enthusiastic that for one shattering moment she thought that he had recognized her, or had mistaken her for someone he knew.

Then her nerves steadied as she realized he was into a well-rehearsed string of patter that he obviously dished up whenever he was showing a female client over a house.

Dennis Jackson really was going to be devastated by what she had planned, she thought smugly as she acknowledged his welcome with a cool smile.

She allowed him to show her over the entire house, enjoying a feeling of power as he exerted every ounce of charm. She pretended to be impressed as he extolled the many advantages to be gained from buying such a property. Then she insisted on seeing the kitchen again. Smiled politely at his whimsical joke about it being 'the heart of the home' and let him precede her down the hallway.

The sand-filled cosh was right on the top of her holdall. When he moved forward to open the door she brought it down on the back of his head with unerring force. His anguished groan was loud, but brief, as he collapsed on to the floor by her feet.

Once she'd checked to make sure he was out cold she'd

slipped the bolts on the front door before starting on the next step of her carefully planned procedure.

Removing her dark-grey suit and her white blouse, she left them in a neat pile on the stairs and changed into what she thought of as her working clothes: black tracksuit bottoms, a black T-shirt, black cagoule and trainers.

Also inside the holdall she'd packed two lengths of stout rope. Using one of these she tied Dennis Jackson's legs together above the ankles and secured the other end of the rope to the door handle. Then she'd tied his wrists with the other piece of rope and fastened the spare end around one of the cupboard doors.

When she was satisfied that he was securely tied down, and unable to move, she looked for something that would hold water. The only thing she could find was a discarded milk bottle, so she filled that from the cold tap and dashed it into Dennis Jackson's face.

His eyelids flickered with shock, and within seconds he was groaning noisily, and staring up utterly confused.

Maureen stood looking down at him. 'Do you remember me, Dennis Jackson?' she asked.

He shook his head. His eyes were bewildered and dark with pain. 'What the hell are you doing to me?' he gasped. 'I've never seen you in my life before.'

'Oh, yes, you have. You may have forgotten, but I haven't! Never for one moment, so think carefully, Dennis Jackson. Think back. Sixteen years ago!'

He winced and closed his eyes as if it was painful to focus them. His breath was coming in quick whining gasps.

Afraid that he might slip back into unconsciousness she refilled the milk bottle with cold water again and stood over him, trickling it on to his face.

He choked and spluttered as it fell into his half-open mouth.

'Come on, try again,' she ordered. 'Benbury Secondary School.'

His eyelids lifted, and the shock in his dark eyes was like that of a trapped animal. 'My God! No . . . it can't be?' He felt as if he was caught up in some terrible nightmare. Her face floated in and out of his mind with every breath he took and every beat of his pulse.

She laughed triumphantly. 'So you do remember!'

'Only that we were at school together,' he mumbled hoarsely.

'Is that all?' Viciously, she jabbed the toe of her trainer into his side. 'Try harder!'

His eyes narrowed. 'What else is there to remember? I'm sure you're not the kid I made pregnant . . . That was Sally Philips.'

She jabbed at him harder, watching him flinch as her trainer made savage contact with his ribs. 'Try thinking about the day when you had the results of your A-levels,' she prompted.

Fear and recognition mingled on his contorted face. 'It's you, isn't it . . . Maureen . . . Maureen Flynn?'

She nodded, her stare never leaving his face.

'So . . . so what are you trying to do? Why tie me up?'

'You tied *me* up.'

'No . . . never! It wasn't me. You're confused.' He tried to bluster, but the impact of her trainer again with the base of his ribs knocked the breath out of him and left him gasping and crying out in agony.

'You not only tied me up, but you encouraged the others who were there in the hut to rape me, and after that you did the most unspeakable things to me,' she reminded him in a savage voice.

'My God! Brian Patterson was right after all,' he groaned. 'He tried to warn me . . . said there was some connection between Sandy's death and John Moorhouse's.'

'And you didn't believe it?' she sneered.

'Why the hell should I? You never said much at the time . . .'

'Because I was petrified by what was happening!'

'But afterwards . . .' His voice grew fainter, and she had to lean closer to catch his words. 'You never did a thing about it then, or said a word to anyone!'

'I told my parents. They were so outraged that my father sold our home and we moved out of Benbury. You ruined their lives as well as mine.'

Dennis Jackson's breathing became more laboured. 'But it all happened years ago . . . nearly twenty,' he protested.

'Sixteen to be exact. And all that time I've hated you, hated myself and felt shamed by what happened to me.'

'We were only kids,' he protested. 'I didn't know any better. We were all high! We'd had too much to drink, and we were excited about passing our exams.'

'I have nightmares about what took place in that shed. I can feel your hands on me, touching me, invading my body. I can hear your voice urging the others to rape me.' Her voice dropped to a sibilant whisper. 'Most of all, Dennis Jackson, I remember the indignities I suffered at your hands.'

He braced himself to make one last plea for forgiveness. 'It was high spirits . . . we were only experimenting.'

The vicious jab of her foot into his solar plexus silenced him.

'Experimenting, were you?' Maureen's lips curled scornfully. 'That's exactly what I'm about to do! Experiment!' She drew a knife out of her brown holdall. 'I'm going to experiment on you, Dennis Jackson, the same as you did on me.'

As she bent over him, wielding the sharp-bladed kitchen knife, he screamed. Quickly, she smothered his cries by clamping the brown holdall hard down on his face.

With his hands and feet tied by ropes, and secured, his struggles were ineffective. He pleaded with his eyes, rolling them from side to side, but Maureen only laughed.

'You always were a dirty bastard, and I don't suppose for one minute that you've changed, so a dose of your own medicine won't come amiss,' she told him disdainfully.

Dennis Jackson writhed in terror as she inserted the tip of the knife inside his shirt, ripped a gaping hole in the material, and then scored a deep gash across the front of his belly.

His eyes bulged, he gasped for breath, tears trickling down his purpling cheeks. He twisted his head from side to side to dislodge the brown bag, but each time he seemed to be about to succeed she rammed it down on his face more firmly.

With tantalizing slowness, she flicked his shirt aside with the point of the knife, then, hooking the knife inside his waistband, sliced his trousers from waist to crotch.

'I want you to appreciate every moment of this,' she told him softly. 'You always enjoyed anything perverted, but this will surpass even your most sadistic dreams,' she promised, kicking the bag away from his face.

He lay snorting and gasping like a beached whale, groaning in agony while his belly contracted, as though racked with cramp or pain. Too late she realized he had lost complete control of his bodily functions.

Exhausted, he lay there in his own filth, howling and screaming like some tormented animal. Bile rose in her throat as the stench infiltrated her nostrils, and she knew she would never be able to erase this moment from her mind.

His eyes now were tightly closed, and because she was afraid he might be drifting off into unconsciousness she dashed another bottle of cold water into his face, making him splutter and choke.

'That's better. I wouldn't want you to miss out on the final stage of my retribution, because I think it's the most exciting piece of the action,' Maureen taunted as she poised the knife tantalizingly above his face. 'Are you ready?'

With a deft movement she bent over him. The knife flashed, plunged, and then made a slashing cut in one swift stroke.

Dennis Jackson's eyes opened so wide that they seemed to encompass his entire face. His mouth gaped as he gave an unearthly scream of mingled pain, panic and outrage that seemed to surge up from deep inside him.

The cry was so terrible that Maureen wanted to clamp her hands over her ears to try and shut it out before it imprinted itself on her brain for ever.

She knew she mustn't do that. If she did, she would lose her nerve, and then she would be unable to finish the task she'd set herself.

It was time for the finale. She must act quickly, before the blood already pumping from his groin defeated the purpose of her final act. Swiftly, before someone outside heard his terrible anguished screams and came to find out what was happening.

Clutching the knife with both hands she plunged it into his belly, into his chest, and then into his throat.

She stepped clear as blood gushed in half a dozen fountains. His glazed eyes stared directly at her as one last choking escaped his lips.

She turned away, temples thumping, head spinning, stomach

churning. Blindly, she stumbled through the kitchen door into the hallway, gasping for air.

Stripping off her black T-shirt, black jogging bottoms, and her trainers, she bundled them into the black plastic bin bag she'd brought with her, along with the knife and lengths of rope.

Naked, she dashed upstairs to the bathroom, where the cold, stinging shower cleansed and revitalized her. Dripping wet, she went downstairs to the hallway and dried herself on her white cotton blouse before putting on the grey suit she'd been wearing when she arrived.

She couldn't bring herself to look again at the body. All she wanted to do was get out of the house.

The other murders she'd committed had left her with a feeling of vengeful pleasure, but this time she was filled with revulsion for what she had done and a feeling of apprehension. She was afraid that at any moment she would lose control.

Thank God there was no one else, she told herself. It wasn't that she felt she had gone too far: it went much deeper than that. It was the tumultuous elation she felt at having accomplished her mission.

Dennis Jackson was the last. She'd saved him until the end because he had been the instigator of what had happened all those years ago, and she'd been determined to inflict on him the ultimate degradation.

And she had! She shuddered as she recalled his maimed, disfigured body.

'He deserved it! And he was the last one!' She repeated it aloud, over and over again, trying desperately to convince herself.

At the back of her mind she wasn't sure. It was true Dennis Jackson had been the instigator of her traumatic sufferings, but the man who had revived those terrible memories had been Philip Harmer.

Could she let him go free? Wasn't he equally as guilty as any of the others?

He was the one who had set in motion this chain of reprisals when he had jilted her. He had incited the desire for revenge that had taken over her life when he had abruptly withdrawn his proposal of marriage.

If only she had gone on guarding her guilty secret instead of complying with his demands. By confessing to everything that had happened in her life prior to meeting him, the humiliation she'd been subjected to when she'd been raped at eighteen, had been revived.

Her head was throbbing, her pulse racing as she drove out of Englefield Drive. At the corner with Barr's Road she narrowly missed a red car, and the realization of what the outcome might have been had they collided made her shake with fright.

Instead of turning out into the main road, Maureen pulled tight into the kerb to take a breather. As she did so, she saw in her rear mirror that the red car had turned into the driveway of the Willows.

Sweat rivered down the nape of her neck. She'd felt so traumatized by the time she was ready to leave the house that she'd found it hard to concentrate, and she wasn't sure if she'd shut the front door securely.

What if she hadn't? Her scalp crawled.

On the brink of panic, and anxious to distance herself from the Willows, she revved the car engine, let out the clutch, and shot out into Barr's Road to a cacophony of horns from other cars as she cut across their path.

She hadn't even noticed if it was a man or a woman driving. She wondered why they had turned into the Willows, since it was empty.

Perhaps it was someone delivering leaflets, she told herself. Even so, if she hadn't shut the door properly, and if they actually went inside, then in a matter of minutes they would raise the alarm and call an ambulance, and probably the police as well.

Once officials arrived on the scene all hell would break loose. There'd be a fearful hue and cry. There was no time to lose. She must decide now what to do. Would it be best to go straight home and lie low, she wondered. She could lock the door, leave the lights off, and pretend she wasn't there.

Or would it be better to make a run for it? Not to go anywhere near her own home, but drive in the opposite direction and carry on until she was a hundred miles or so away from Benbury and Dutton?

Where would she stay if she did that, though? She didn't want to spend the night in her car, and she could hardly book into a reputable hotel without a suitcase.

Maureen was suddenly filled with a sense of impending disaster. Even at this moment the police might be setting up road blocks. Supposing they stopped her and asked to look in the boot of her car!

She felt a tightening in her throat. The moment they saw the bulky black bin bag they'd be suspicious. And once they looked inside it that would be the end!

She drove faster anxious to put as many miles as possible between herself and Benbury before the police started to take action.

Her nerves felt raw. Her left eye was twitching so fast that she had to keep putting her hand over it. She'd planned Dennis Jackson's murder with such care and precision that she refused to believe it was all going to go wrong. She'd felt such elation when she'd turned into the driveway of the Willows and seen the dark-green Mercedes pulled up in front of the house, and known that Dennis Jackson was already there waiting for her.

She shook her head, like a dog coming out of the river, trying to clear the kaleidoscope of memories. The important thing now, she told herself, was to concentrate on the present. She must decide where she was going, and how she was going to dispose of the black plastic bag of incriminating evidence that was in the boot of her car before she was stopped by the police and interrogated.

SEVENTEEN

'Calm down, Miss Lowe. If we are to catch the person who carried out this dreadful crime we need your help.' Ruth spoke in a low, soothing tone. 'I want you to try and tell us exactly what happened.'

June Lowe's grey eyes were wide with fear as she looked from Inspector Morgan to Sergeant Hardcastle and back again.

'I don't know what happened . . . I wasn't here . . . I found him like . . . like . . .'

'And you say you found the front door open when you arrived?' queried Paddy.

'Yes!' Her voice was barely a whisper.

'Why were you here?'

'I . . . I came to remind Mr Jackson that he had promised his wife he'd be home early.'

'So you expected to find him here?'

'I . . . I wasn't sure. I knew he'd come here earlier to show a client round—'

'And the client's name?' interrupted Paddy.

June lifted her shapely shoulders in a hopeless shrug. 'I can't remember. Metcalfe . . . or Maitland.' Her face brightened. 'Yes, that was it. Maitland. Margaret Maitland.'

'Would you know this woman if you saw her again?'

June Lowe shook her head. 'She made the appointment over the phone . . . She didn't come into the office.'

'So you haven't an address? You hadn't sent her details of the property?'

June shook her head.

'So you knew Mr Jackson was coming here to show this woman around, and so you dropped in on your way home from work to remind him he was supposed to be home early.'

'Yes. That's right.'

'Couldn't you have phoned him?'

'I did try to get him on his mobile! There isn't a phone

connected in the house . . . It's been empty for quite some time.'

'And you got no reply from his mobile,' repeated Paddy.

'No. I tried more than once. And I phoned his home, but I couldn't get a reply from there either. Mrs Jackson must have gone out and forgotten to leave the answerphone on.'

'So you came here to remind him about his promise to be home early, and you found the door was open.'

'Not wide open. Just off the catch. As though someone hadn't closed it properly.'

'And you thought Mr Jackson might still be inside.'

'His car was in the drive so I thought that the client had left and he was locking up. Quite often they want to go outside and look around the garden so you have to open the back door, or the patio doors,' she explained.

'So what did you do when you found the door ajar?'

'I rang the bell, knocked on the door and then walked into the hallway and called out his name.'

'And when there was no answer?'

'I didn't know what to do. I knew he wouldn't have gone and left the front door open. He's a stickler about doors. He always gives them a shake after he's locked them to make quite sure they're secure. In the case of an unoccupied house we are responsible for its security once it's on our books, you see.'

'Right. And then what happened?'

June Lowe's face crumpled, and she dabbed at her eyes with a screwed up tissue.

Ruth gently patted the girl's arm. 'Try and tell us . . . in your own words,' she murmured.

'Well, I went into the hall, as far as the stairs, and I called out his name again. Then I went into the kitchen . . .' She gulped and held a hand over her mouth as if she was about to be sick.

'And that was where you found Mr Jackson . . . on the floor by the sink?'

June Lowe shuddered and nodded. 'It was terrible,' she said, gulping.

'Go on!'

'He . . . he was lying stretched straight out . . . There was blood . . . blood on his face . . . and on . . . and on his clothes.' Her voice became a whisper. 'His clothes . . . His shirt had been ripped open and . . . and . . .'

Unable to go on, she covered her face with her hands.

'So what did you do then?' Paddy asked tersely.

June Lowe was crying so much that her words were unintelligible. Ruth signalled to him to wait until the girl had control of herself.

When her anguished sobbing had tapered down to mere sniffles, he repeated his question. 'So what did you do then?'

'I ran to my car and rang you,' said June Lowe.

'Why did you do that? Surely you had your mobile in your handbag with you!'

Fresh tears welled up in her eyes and coursed down her cheeks. 'I . . . I don't know. I knew I must get help . . . I wanted to get out of the house . . . away . . . away from his body.'

'Don't worry about it,' Ruth reassured her. 'Simply tell it as it happened. She flashed a warning signal at Paddy. His terse questions were not helping.

'I stayed in my car until the police came,' June Lowe went on, looking at Ruth. 'They brought me back to the house with them. Then the ambulance arrived, and more police . . . and . . . and then you came and started questioning me!' Her voice rose hysterically. 'I've told you all I know. I want to go home. I don't know anything else. I don't know what happened. I've told you everything, and now can I go?'

Paddy shook his head. 'There are still a lot more questions . . .'

'Please . . . please not now!' June Lowe implored, clutching at his sleeve.

He shot a glance at Ruth, and she shook her head, an imperceptible warning that she thought the girl had been through enough for the moment.

'Very well,' he said stiffly. 'We'll send you home in a police car, but you will have to come to the station tomorrow for further questioning.'

She hesitated, shaking her head. 'I have my own car . . .'

'But you're in no fit condition to drive it,' he snapped.

'Would it be possible for someone to drive me home, then? My mother wouldn't like it if I was brought home in a police car.'

'There didn't seem to be much point in questioning her any further while she is so overwrought,' Ruth commented once Paddy had arranged for June Lowe to be taken home.

'No. Probably not, ma'am,' he said coldly.

'It's hardly likely she did it, or that she knows who was responsible.'

'She was driving a red car though!' he pointed out smugly.

'We're looking for a red Ford Escort and her car wasn't a Ford.'

'Are we? One of the witnesses wasn't at all certain that it was an Escort – only that it was a red car.'

Ruth let it pass. She was more concerned with the forensic report. Although Dennis Jackson's murder bore a great many of the same hallmarks as the three previous murders, there were also several marked differences.

This time the murderer hadn't been content to merely disarrange the victim's clothes to simulate sexual interference but had gone a step further and actually carried out a serious mutilation of the man's genitals.

In addition, there were marks on his wrists and around his ankles that indicated they had been tied together with rope. There was also a massive bruise on the back of Dennis Jackson's head which did not conform with him having banged his head on the floor through a fall.

An hour later, the evidence they'd obtained was even more grisly.

'As a rough reconstruction,' Paddy said, 'I'd say that he was coshed on the head, then trussed up, with his hands tied together and fastened to something in the kitchen. His feet were also tied together and fastened to something else in the room, so that he was stretched out so straight that he'd be in agony. After that, I'm not sure. Obviously that was when his clothing was ripped and when . . . when he was mutilated. The most sadistic thing I've ever witnessed,' he added in a tone of utter distaste.

'The work of a man . . . a husband who has been double crossed by Jackson,' mused Ruth.

'No! Never!' Paddy looked almost offended. 'A man wouldn't do anything as sadistic as that!'

'If he was very much in love with his wife; if he wanted her back; if he hated the fellow's guts for breaking up his marriage,' listed Ruth.

'Then he'd punch the fellow's head in, shoot him, even, but not stab him and mutilate him like that.'

Ruth studied him dispassionately. She had never seen Paddy so incensed. She'd thought of him as mild mannered, slow to rouse. Intelligent but not brilliant, pleasant but not complex. Which, she mused, was probably why he'd been passed over when it came to promotion.

'So you're suggesting it was a woman who did this?'

Paddy stroked his chin thoughtfully. 'She would have to be either very strong or else so enraged that she had abnormal strength. In the normal way, all these men would be able to fight off a woman.'

'Unless they were taken by surprise,' argued Ruth. 'The first three were all concentrating on what they were doing when they were stabbed from behind.'

'Dennis Jackson looks as though he was attacked from behind with a heavy blunt instrument . . .'

'But we can't be sure if that was what killed him.'

'True!' Paddy conceded reluctantly.

'This murder differs in quite a number of ways from the others—'

'That is what is so worrying,' interrupted Paddy. 'If the killer coshed him from behind, then why stab him in the chest? Unless it was to make sure that it was linked to the others?'

Ruth looked thoughtful. 'Yes, I suppose that is a possibility.'

'In which case we have to consider this a copycat murder and not as the work of a serial killer.'

'Unless he was only knocked unconscious and when he came round . . .' Her voice trailed off as she met Paddy's eyes.

The thought uppermost in both their minds was: had the man been stabbed to death before being mutilated?

If it had happened the other way round – that he had been mutilated first and then stabbed to death – then they were looking for a highly dangerous, sadistic psychopath.

'Time of death appears to have been between four o' clock and six o'clock. We know that from the fact that Dennis Jackson left his office just before four to keep an appointment with a woman called Margaret Maitland—'

'Mrs or miss?' interrupted Paddy.

'We don't know. We could ask June Lowe.'

'And when she's had time to calm down let's hope she can give us a more detailed description of the woman.'

'She won't be able to do that. The woman phoned in.'

'Then it might be worth checking with the people who live in the adjacent houses. Someone may have seen her arrive.'

The houses in Englefield Drive were not only detached but all of them were very individual, and they all had long drives and ample gardens separating them from their neighbours. Many, like the Willows, had such high, dense hedges that it was almost impossible to see into each other's gardens.

Detective Inspector Ruth Morgan and Detective Sergeant Paddy Hardcastle obtained only one clue as the result of several interviews. The woman whose property adjoined the Willows on the right-hand side told them that a red car had pulled into the driveway just before four o'clock.

She had been in her garden and had been interested because only five minutes earlier she had seen Dennis Jackson's car arrive, and she thought the occupant of the red car might be a prospective new neighbour.

She'd still been in the garden an hour later when the red car drove away. She was unable to tell them whether or not it was a Ford Escort or if it had been a man or woman behind the wheel.

A teenage boy reported that he had seen a small red car, and he was pretty sure it was a Mini, turning into the Willows when he'd been delivering evening newspapers around six o'clock, shortly before the police arrived.

'That was June Lowe's car, of course,' said Paddy with a sigh as he checked over his notes.

'You don't suppose it was her car that was there earlier?'

'I doubt it. According to what she told us, she was at the office until almost six o' clock, remember.' He frowned and shuffled the papers in front of him. 'Not unless *she* did the murder!'

Ruth shook her head. 'She was upset when we arrived, but she showed no evidence of having been in any way involved . . .'

'She would have had time to go home, change her clothes, and then come back again.'

'That would have taken tremendous nerve!'

'Even so, we'd better send someone round to check out everything she was wearing, right down to her shoes, before she has time to dispose of any of them.'

'And what was her connection with the other murders?'

Paddy shrugged. 'Perhaps they're not connected. If we can solve one of them it will help to keep Superintendent Wilson off our backs.'

Ruth shook her head. 'I think we are going round in circles, and not only that, I think we're on the wrong trail. It might be better if we went to see Mrs Jackson, to find out if she can throw some light on the matter.'

Deborah Jackson answered the door in a stunning black velvet dress, sheer black stockings and high-heeled court shoes. Her make-up was flawless, and it was obvious she was all ready for a special evening out.

Her green eyes grew bright with unshed tears, and she pushed back her shoulder-length hair in a dramatic gesture of shock and despair when they broke the news of her husband's murder to her.

He had all the attributes of a saint as she described him to Ruth and Paddy. She painted a glowing picture of a devoted husband – not a man who flirted outrageously with almost every woman he met.

Because Paddy was a local man, and knew Dennis Jackson's reputation, he disbelieved almost every word she uttered and wondered why she was so very much on the defensive. He questioned her, and soon the truth came out, amidst floods of tears.

'You surely don't think she had any part in her husband's murder?' Ruth queried, after they'd spent a gruelling hour listening to Deborah Jackson's diatribe.

'She had every cause to murder him,' Paddy told her dryly. 'Even as a schoolboy he had a reputation as a sexually devious monster!'

'I suppose she could have arranged it,' mused Ruth. 'Even have planned it so that it fitted into the same pattern as the other three murders . . .'

'. . . and had it carried out by a hired killer? Now that's a thought. That would account for the many similarities.'

'And for the variances which don't fit into the previous pattern?'

'You mean the fact that he had been coshed and tied up as well as stabbed? It would need a man to exert that sort of strength, wouldn't it?'

'But you said you couldn't conceive any man carrying out that sort of mutilation,' Ruth reminded him.

'Perhaps we're not looking for just one person. It could be a couple. The man strikes the blow . . . the woman does the mutilations!'

EIGHTEEN

Detective Superintendent James Wilson was beside himself with anger. Judging from the contents of the Home Office letter he was reading, he was in no doubt that heads would roll unless some positive progress was made on the Benbury murders.

From the tone of the letter, he suspected that even his own position was in jeopardy unless there were satisfactory developments in the immediate future.

It had been a mistake to put Detective Inspector Ruth Morgan in charge of the case, he reflected. Not because she was a woman. He wasn't sexist. But she had come in through what his generation would describe as the back door.

First-class university honours and Police Training College were all very well, but it wasn't the same as hands-on experience. That was why he had assigned Paddy as her sergeant. Paddy was a product of the old school. He'd started on the beat, and worked himself up by study, and practical application. He had an invaluable wealth of experience.

James Wilson sighed aloud. If he'd been able to convince the board to think the same way as himself, the post of detective inspector would have gone to Paddy.

The position could still be his if Inspector Morgan didn't shape up, he thought grimly as he opened the file containing all the information so far assembled on the Benbury murders.

Detective Inspector Ruth Morgan waited in trepidation to be summoned to Superintendent Wilson's office. He had become increasingly tetchy with each new murder, and this fourth one would further justify his unspoken criticism that she wasn't right for the job.

She only hoped that Dennis Jackson wasn't another personal friend of the inspector's, or a fellow Mason. Since he was a prominent local businessman, owner of the largest estate agency in Benbury, it was more than likely that he was both, she thought gloomily.

If only there were more clues. At present she could list what little they knew about this murder, and the three earlier ones, on one side of a piece of paper!

A red car that could be a Ford Escort, a Vauxhall or even a Mini had all been seen in the vicinity of one or the other of the murders. There was a hard to define logo taken from the instep imprint of a trainer. A parking ticket from the car park near the Masonic hall where the second murder had taken place, the time and date so blurred that they hadn't been able to ascertain when it had been issued.

Hardly the sort of evidence to convict a serial killer on, she thought ruefully. The only other deducible link was that all the victims were the same age, and they'd all attended Benbury Secondary School. She had sent Paddy along to the school to see if they could turn up the attendance registers for twenty years ago and check who else had been in the same class, to see if that offered any lead.

As the owner of the largest newsagent's in Benbury, Sandy Franklin was known to at least half the town's population. Brian Patterson, they had discovered, was not only Sandy Franklin's solicitor, but he also undertook property conveyancing for Dennis Jackson. John Moorhouse seemed to be the odd one out. Although he'd been at school with the others, none of them seemed to be linked to him. He didn't move in the same circles as any of them. And yet he had been the first to be murdered.

Ruth found it puzzling. She wondered if this was some sort of clue. If she could establish the link between Moorhouse and the others would it lead her to the killer? Always assuming that it *was* the same person who had carried out all the attacks. Namely, a serial killer. If they were copycat killings then they really were in trouble. It might even mean they were looking for four murderers!

She didn't think they were, though. Even the last killing followed the same basic pattern as the three previous ones. It was more sadistic, though. As if the killer had reached a peak, a crescendo of madness that had carried the murders into the realms of atrocity.

Ruth shuffled through the papers, picking out anything she could find that related to the four wives – or, in Sandy Franklin's case, to his most recent girlfriend, Tracey Walker – convinced that there must be a link there somewhere, some vital clue that she was overlooking.

She spread the information out on her desk in four separate piles and studied them. All the women seemed to have known Sandy Franklin – along with half the female population of Benbury, if rumours were to be believed, she thought dryly. So was there any evidence against any of them?

On the night Marilyn Moorhouse's husband had been murdered she had been wearing black jeans and trainers, which Forensic reported had no blood stains on them, and the trainers didn't tally in any way with the imprint they'd found.

Tracey Walker had appeared genuinely surprised and distressed by the news of Sandy Franklin's murder. She had apparently been in bed when he'd left and had not heard anything at all suspicious. Furthermore, Ruth reflected, the flat had revealed no trace of a disturbance.

Had she followed Sandy Franklin out of the flat when he left, stabbed him, and then dashed back indoors, changed her clothes, and been able to act surprised when the police arrived to alert her that he had been killed?

It seemed unlikely, Ruth decided. What could Tracey have gained by killing her boyfriend? It was far more probable that Mrs Agnes Walker had been waiting outside when he left the flat, and that she had been the one to stab him. Except that she had been able to account for her movements on the evening in question, while Tracey could not. Agnes' alibi was absolutely watertight. She could produce a dozen witnesses to the fact that she'd been in Dorset, over a hundred miles away.

Sara Patterson didn't seem to be the type to murder her husband, either, although she had been extremely evasive about why she had been absent from home the night her husband had been murdered.

She also favoured jeans and trainers for everyday wear when taking her two small daughters to school, but neither her shoe size, nor the manufacturer's logo, fitted with the one footprint they had as evidence.

Ruth would have liked to eliminate her name altogether from the list of suspects, but since Sara Patterson did drive a small red car she was afraid it might be considered precipitous by Superintendent Wilson, and one thing she couldn't afford to do was antagonize the superintendent by letting it appear that her investigations didn't explore every possible avenue.

Like Deborah Jackson!

Ruth sighed deeply as she picked up the sheaf of papers relating to the wife of the latest victim. From the information gleaned it would appear that Deborah Jackson was a lady who had some very good reasons for murdering her virile, handsome husband.

After some initial reticence, Deborah Jackson had made no secret of the fact that her husband was a womanizer. She'd also admitted that this time matters had reached a point between her and her husband when she intended to ask him to decide between her and his latest paramour, a Spanish lady named Martina Carpenter.

Had one of Dennis Jackson's discarded mistresses been the mysterious Margaret Maitland who had phoned the Jackson Estate Agency under the pretence of wishing to see over the Willows in Englefield Drive so that she could meet him there?

That had been the second time that an eyewitness had reported seeing a red car in the vicinity immediately following one of the murders. Only this time they insisted it had been a small car, possibly a Mini.

Ruth tabulated the various sightings of red cars the vicinity of each murder. The woman who had been in her garden next door in Englefield Drive had claimed to have seen a red car follow Dennis Jackson's green Mercedes into the driveway of the Willows at around four o' clock. She had also seen it leave about an hour later, and she thought it had possibly been the same red car that had returned at about six o' clock.

They had checked out the times and knew that the six o'clock caller had been June Lowe, Dennis Jackson's PA. Her car was red, and since the woman was unsure of the make Ruth wondered if the woman had confused the two different cars and thought it was the same one each time.

So had it been June Lowe the first time? Had she lured her

boss to the Willows, knowing it was an empty house, killed him, driven away, and then returned again an hour later on the pretext of telling him his wife wanted him to be home early?

But why come back? Could it have been in order to assuage her conscience? Or even to make sure he was discovered?

Perhaps she hadn't meant to kill him and thought if she raised the alarm, and he was 'found' in time, he would be rushed to hospital and recover.

Remembering the nature of his wounds, and their severity, Ruth thought that was highly unlikely. She gathered up the papers she had spread out over her desk and stacked them up into a neat pile. It was no good. She was getting nowhere, simply going round in circles.

She picked up her suit jacket, which she had removed and hung over the back of her chair. Perhaps a cup of canteen coffee might help clear her brain. And by then Paddy might be back, and he might have discovered some background link from the four men's schooldays that might throw some light on to why they had been killed. Even if he hadn't, then she'd test out her own theories on him, and that might lead to something.

She felt it undermined her authority having to depend on him so much, but he had grown up in Benbury; he knew things about these people that she didn't. It also gave him an advantage when he was interviewing suspects. Because he was a local man, they seemed to open up to him more than to her. As if they trusted him. They seemed to be suspicious of her motives, and that put them on their guard.

As she collected a mug of coffee from the dispenser in the canteen and carried it across to a window seat, she wondered if Paddy thought of her as an outsider. Would he have been more cooperative if she had been a local person, even though she was his superior, she mused as she sat with both hands around the mug.

She knew it was partly her own fault. The first few days she had been at Benbury he had been almost chummy. He'd gone out of his way to be helpful! She'd rebuffed him. She hadn't been cool; in fact, she'd been absolutely icy!

Superintendent Wilson had told her when he'd assigned Paddy as her sergeant that he was the most knowledgeable and experienced CID officer in the Benbury force. She had expected a grim-faced man in his late fifties, not someone only in his thirties who was tall, broad shouldered and handsome into the bargain, with vivid blue eyes and a slow, contagious smile.

When she'd learnt that he was a bachelor she had let him know, right from the start, that she held the higher rank, and that she was his boss. She didn't want him to think he could chat her up as he might any rookie policewoman. Now that she knew him better she realized that he was far too much the professional to think of doing such a thing.

He'd been quick to read the signs, she'd say that much in his favour. When she'd declined to even have a coffee with him when they were on duty, his manner towards her had changed immediately. He'd remained courteous but distant. There was absolutely nothing she could fault in his manner, but she suspected he wasn't going out of his way to draw on his local expertise, even though he must know that it might make their job a whole lot easier if he did. He seemed to respond to the superintendent more than he did to her!

She frowned and took another mouthful of coffee as a germ of suspicion circled in her mind. Was that deliberate, she wondered. Was Paddy trying to make a point, trying to show Superintendent Wilson that he would have made a better detective inspector than her, and that he should have been promoted?

She drained her mug of coffee. She couldn't let that happen. Her career was on the line; her ability to prove herself depended on the way she handled this case.

It was imperative that she had Paddy's full cooperation; essential that they worked as a team in solving the Benbury murders, she decided grimly.

She would have to convince him that teamwork was in both their interests. She would start by changing her attitude towards him, she resolved.

NINETEEN

Detective Sergeant Paddy Hardcastle left Benbury Secondary School feeling satisfied yet mystified by what he had found out. The headmaster had been most helpful. He had introduced him to Mr Perks, the head of history, an elderly man on the point of retirement, who had been a teacher at the school for over twenty-five years. Mr Perks had been able to give him a great deal of useful information about the four men who had been murdered.

As he entered Benbury Police Station, Paddy didn't go straight to the CID office, but made his way to the canteen. Although he'd already had a coffee during his visit to Benbury Secondary School, he wanted time to sit and think about what he had learned before passing the information on to Inspector Morgan.

It irked him that he had to hand over the information he had gleaned to someone else and let them make the decisions as to what action should be taken. With his qualifications, and length of service, he should have been made up to inspector, and then he would be the one in charge of this investigation, he thought irritably.

It was all very well Inspector Ruth Morgan talking about team spirit, but she would be the one to receive all the accolades when they solved the case!

Not that there had been much success so far, but he was quietly confident that with the new evidence he'd just collected it would only be a matter of time before the culprit was apprehended.

Inspector Morgan was a nice enough person, quite attractive in a way, but she wasn't local, and as someone born and bred in Benbury he felt he had a greater empathy with the people who lived in the town than she did.

And it was all very well Superintendent James Wilson having a man to man talk with him about giving her his full support, and saying that he was relying on him to help her to settle in, but *he* wasn't the one who had been cheated out of his rightful promotion. Without his local knowledge, inspector or not, she'd get nowhere!

He wouldn't have minded if Inspector Morgan had been a little more friendly. He knew she was new to her rank, new to the police force if it came to that, but she didn't have to make it quite so obvious that she was his superior. Some of the inspectors he'd worked with before were as matey as you like when they were out in the car. They'd laugh and crack a joke, exchange gossip, and even share a packet of fish and chips with you. They knew you'd not let them down in front of the super, or when you were doing interviews. They knew they could rely on you to show the correct deference, call them sir, and all that sort of thing, when it was appropriate to do so.

Ruth Morgan acted more like a headmistress than a colleague. It was as if because she wasn't in uniform, with an insignia on her shoulder to show her rank, she constantly had to impress on him that she was his superior.

He wondered if she was a feminist. Or a lesbian, even, the way she sat so prim and straight in the squad car as if she was afraid that if their knees touched, or his hand brushed against hers, he might suddenly rape her.

If she was more relaxed, if her mouth was less hard and grim, and her dark eyes lost that suspicious look whenever he spoke to her, she might be quite attractive. It would certainly make working together a whole lot easier!

He collected a cup of coffee from the machine and was making his way across the room to find a window seat when he pulled up short. He couldn't believe his eyes. Detective Inspector Ruth Morgan was sitting in the canteen, drinking coffee! She was on her own, staring into space as though deep in thought, and for a moment he thought of edging quietly away, hoping she hadn't seen him. How was he going to explain away the fact that he was taking time off to drink coffee when she was probably on tenterhooks waiting to find out if his visit to the school had drummed up any new evidence?

He grinned to himself. She was there drinking coffee herself, wasn't she? Perhaps she was human after all and under that frozen exterior she was a normal warm-blooded woman.

Now was the time to find out!

'When you weren't in your office I wondered if I would find you in here, ma'am,' he greeted her, setting his cup down on the table. 'Can I get you a refill?'

When she hesitated, he said quickly, 'I can tell you what I've found out this afternoon while we drink our coffee, if you like.'

Again she hesitated, biting down on her lower lip before finally nodding in agreement.

'I take it your visit was worthwhile,' she commented as he set the steaming mug of coffee down in front of her.

'Yes, it was. The head was most cooperative, but equally important there was a teacher there who had taught all four of the murder victims.'

'Really!'

'He remembered them quite well. It seems all four of them managed to get A-level passes. Out of a class of fifteen there were only six pupils that year who managed to achieve this . . .'

'Six? And four of them are dead . . .' Ruth's voice trailed away.

Paddy took a gulp of his coffee. He was pretty sure he knew what she was thinking. In fact, he'd been thinking much the same himself ever since he'd left the school.

'Could he remember the names of the other two pupils?'

'Not offhand, but he's promised to let me have the list.'

'When?' Her tone was sharp, impatient.

'Today if he can find it. All the old records are stored in the basement. He promised to send the janitor down there to unearth it . . .'

'Sergeant Hardcastle!'

Their conversation was interrupted by a uniformed constable. 'There's a Mr Perks asking for you at the front desk. He said he spoke to you earlier today. He says it's important.'

'I'll be right out!' Paddy drained the last of his coffee. 'Perks is the history teacher I was telling you about. He's probably brought that list along.'

Ruth stood up. 'Would you mind if I had a word with him?'

Her manner was more conciliatory than it had been since they'd met, so he nodded. 'Of course! I'll bring him along to your office.'

Mr Perks was a thin upright man in his early sixties with iron grey hair and dark bushy eyebrows that framed a pair of intense dark eyes. Dressed in a slate blue suit, light blue shirt with a shiny white collar, and wearing a royal blue tie that exactly matched the handkerchief peeping out of the breast pocket of his jacket, he looked both academic and formidable.

He greeted Sergeant Hardcastle effusively and at once launched into a description of the contents of the package he was carrying. For a moment he looked irritated when Paddy interrupted his flow of words in order to introduce him to Ruth.

'DI Morgan is in charge of the case,' Paddy explained, emphasizing the word 'Inspector'.

'Oh, I see!' Mr Perks looked a little taken aback. 'Then I had better go back to the beginning and start again . . . unless you have already relayed the information I gave you earlier today?'

'Sergeant Hardcastle has told me the basic facts,' Ruth told him, 'but I'd like to hear it all again . . . in your own words.'

'Right! All four of the men who have been killed over the past few weeks were once pupils in the same class at Benbury Secondary School.'

'How many were there taking their A-levels, Mr Perks?'

'Only fifteen. Most of the pupils left once they had their O-levels. And out of those fifteen who remained there were only six who passed their A-levels. The four men who've been killed and two other pupils.'

'Do you think it at all possible that there's some link?'

Mr Perks looked from Sergeant Hardcastle to Inspector Morgan and back again. 'I have no idea!' He regarded them from over the top of his glasses. 'That is for you to decide. Perhaps this will help.' He drew the package he had placed on the table nearer to him and began to unwrap it.

Paddy moved closer, and side by side with Ruth, bent over

the table to examine the register that Mr Perks was unwrapping.

In a typical schoolmasterish way, Mr Perks displayed the list of pupils who had formed the A-level class of 1977. With slow deliberation he pointed out the names of the four victims: Moorhouse, Franklin, Patterson and Jackson.

Then he pointed to two other names: Gould and Flynn.

'Those two were also A-level achievers,' he informed DI Morgan and DS Hardcastle as he peered at them again from over the top of his glasses.

Ruth and Paddy exchanged glances and it was obvious to both of them that their thoughts were running on parallel lines.

'Gould and Flynn will have to be found, questioned and warned,' Ruth told Mr Perks. 'We might even consider offering them some form of protection.'

'Yes, I thought that might be the case, which is why I have brought along a couple of school photographs, taken on the last day of term,' Mr Perks stated.

Rather like a conjuror producing a rabbit from an empty hat, he produced two framed photographs. 'This one is a group of the entire class. The other one is of the six achievers.'

'A photograph showing the remaining two . . .' breathed Ruth in disbelief. This was more than she dared dream about. At last, some concrete evidence to lay before Superintendent Wilson.

The photographs had been taken sixteen years earlier, and her immediate elation was slightly dampened when she gazed at the youthful faces of the six who had passed their A-levels. 'Moorhouse, Franklin, Patterson, Jackson . . .' She spoke the names out loud as her finger moved over the photograph identifying each one. Then she stopped in surprise. 'Mr Perks, one of these is a girl!'

'Yes. That's right. Maureen Flynn. She was the star pupil that year. She achieved the highest results of them all,' Mr Perks stated.

'Did she go on to university?'

Mr Perks shook his head. 'Not as far as I know, but I can't be certain. Her family left Benbury shortly afterwards, and I'm afraid I have no idea what happened to her.'

'And the other boy?'

'Aah. Now, his name was Gould. Simon Gould. He became involved with cars and motor racing.' He scowled. 'Silly young fool! He had an excellent brain . . . leastways, he did before the accident.'

'Accident?' Ruth asked.

'Yes, he was involved in a serious smash on one of the race tracks. It made headline news at the time. There was something about the car being faulty, and if I remember correctly he sued either the company he worked for, or the manufacturers, for a colossal amount of compensation.'

'And what happened to him after that?'

'I'm not sure,' Mr Perks said.

'I remember the case. The papers were full of it at the time,' Paddy said thoughtfully. 'He was in hospital for months, wasn't he?'

'For about three months, I believe.'

'I remember reading about his fight for compensation. As you say, he got a very substantial sum, and I think someone told me he bought a garage.'

'In Benbury?' Ruth asked.

'No, not locally. He felt very sensitive about the fact that he was facially disfigured and moved away from Benbury. He wanted to start afresh where no one would know him.'

'He always was very headstrong,' Mr Perks commented disapprovingly.

'Maureen Flynn and Simon Gould,' Ruth murmured thoughtfully. She smiled at Mr Perks. 'You have been most helpful. Would you mind if we kept these items? I promise you we'll take great care of them,' she added quickly as she saw the look of hesitation on his lined face.

'And you will be sure to return them afterwards? They are part of the school archives, you see. The head was rather reluctant for me to bring them here. He didn't really approve of them being removed from the school premises.'

'We quite understand. We'll take the greatest care of them and return them to you as soon as our enquiries are completed.

Ruth left Paddy to see Mr Perks out. When he returned to

the office he found she was still studying the photograph of the six Benbury Secondary School students.

'Perhaps we should have a blow-up of Gould and the girl circulated,' he suggested.

She looked doubtful. 'Would it help? These pictures were taken sixteen years ago. Neither of them will look the same now. Gould certainly won't bear much resemblance to this picture, not after his car accident.'

'Someone might remember them as they were, and come forward, and tell us where they are today.'

'That's possible, I suppose. The only thing is if we do circulate these pictures, and one of them is the murderer, they'll know right away that we are on to them.'

'That's true!'

She frowned. 'I have a gut feeling that it's the girl, Maureen Flynn, who is involved in some way.'

'You mean she might be the murderer?'

'The few clues we have point to it being a woman.'

Paddy looked dubious. 'The red car and the parking ticket could belong to a man or woman.'

'Forensic said they thought that the trainer was a woman's because of the size.'

'It might account for the strange sexual deviation attached to all the murders,' Paddy mused.

'And the methods used in each case.'

'You mean the surprise attacks so that the victim had no opportunity of defending himself?'

'Precisely! After all, as you said, a woman probably wouldn't have the physical strength to overpower a man.'

For the first time since they had started the investigation Ruth felt they were getting somewhere. 'Maureen Flynn was the one who achieved top A-level results that year,' she pointed out. 'That must have made her feel special, equal to the five boys.'

'Do you mean she was jealous of them?' queried Paddy, unable to see which way her argument was going.

'Not jealous. She knew she was as good as them. No, I think her feelings went deeper than that . . .'

'You mean you think she was in love with one of them,

and he rejected her, and now, all these years later, she is taking some sort of revenge?'

Ruth shook her head. 'I don't know about that. I don't pretend to understand what the real motive is behind these killings, but I am sure it relates to something that happened between her and those boys.'

'Hmm!' Paddy rubbed a hand over his chin thoughtfully. 'In that case we'd better locate Simon Gould and warn him that he may be in danger, don't you?'

TWENTY

gnoring the darkness closing in around her, Maureen Flynn instinctively drove north-west without stopping, until the petrol gauge on her Ford Escort registered NIL. Even then she kept on going, the engine spluttering, choked by dirt from the bottom of the sump.

She knew that unless she pulled in for petrol within the next few minutes she would find herself stranded by the roadside, and she hadn't the slightest idea where she was.

Knowing she had bungled the last killing clouded her brain. Whoever it was that had been driving the red Mini she'd almost collided with in Englefield Drive, and who had turned into the Willows, couldn't have helped but find Dennis Jackson's body – and by now they must have informed the police.

She was surprised that she had not encountered any road blocks. She'd been expecting at any minute to hear the wail of police sirens and find a panda car alongside her, signalling her to pull over.

The fear of this happening was why she was so intent on putting as many miles as possible between herself and Benbury.

Yet she needed to stop, and not only for petrol. She was ravenously hungry, and her throat so dry that it was painful to breathe.

Normally, food didn't bother her a great deal. She ate sparingly, but now she had an overwhelming yearning for fish and chips. Fish and chips wrapped up in paper! The chips soaked in vinegar. Eating them with her fingers.

There was one other compelling reason why she must stop, and that was to get rid of the bulky black bin bag stowed in the boot of her car.

A council refuse tip was the only safe place to dispose of that! There she could throw it into one of the huge skips where, in next to no time, it would be buried under garden refuse and other rubbish. That was what she had done with all the others.

No one would ever find any of them. The skips would be emptied straight on to the burning grounds, and, once the contents were incinerated the evidence would be gone forever without trace.

She'd feel so much calmer once the bag was out of her car. Then she'd be safe! Even if she was intercepted by the police there would be no evidence to connect her with the murder. It was madness not to have stopped before this and got rid of it, she told herself. Probably all the tips would be closed at this time of night, but even if the gates were locked she might be able to toss the bag over them into the nearest skip.

Frantically, she checked the fuel gauge. The needle had slipped down below the red warning panel. Unless she filled up with petrol soon she'd never reach a council tip.

Petrol. PETROL. PETROL! The word hammered on her brain.

She wondered what time it was. The clock in the car showed it was almost eight o'clock, but she couldn't believe it was that late. She tried to see the time by her watch, but it was too dark inside the car to do so.

She should have stuck to the main road – used the motorway, even. Then she would have found plenty of service stations where she could have filled up, and she would also have been able to get a drink and some food.

It was no good thinking about that now, Maureen told herself. She had no idea where she was except that it was a minor road somewhere in remote countryside. There was bound to be a road sign soon, at the next crossroads, or the next junction with a main road, she thought. When she did find one, however, the names on it meant nothing to her. She had twisted and turned so much that she was obviously in some very minor country road, and the roads off it were tracks to outlying cottages or houses.

A feeling of panic surged through her. The mountainous clouds in the darkening sky took on terrifying shapes. She could hear her own harsh breathing as the hedgerows seemed to close in on her. When she suddenly came to another road junction, and turned out on to what was obviously a main road, her relief was intense, and when she spotted the illuminated sign of a petrol station a few hundred yards down the road she wondered if it was real or a figment of her tormented mind.

As she pulled on to the forecourt the engine gave one final splutter and died. Maureen didn't know whether to laugh with relief because a fill-up was so close, or cry with despair because it was obvious the hose from the petrol pump wasn't going to reach the filler on her car.

A man with a heavy dark beard appeared from the workshop that stood at one side and as he came towards her she noticed he had a pronounced limp.

'Cut it a bit fine, didn't you? I heard you spluttering down the road, and I wondered if you'd make it.'

'Thank heaven I found you open! Do you think you could give me a push?'

'You sit tight and steer,' he told her.

'Thanks!'

By the time he'd filled the tank up Maureen was feeling more in control of herself. 'Can you tell me what the nearest town is?' she asked as she paid for the petrol.

'Depends which way you're going!' He guffawed at his own joke. 'This is Pontydaren. Builth Wells is that way, and Brecon is that way. You're about halfway between the two.'

She looked startled. 'You mean I'm in Wales?'

He laughed. 'Where did you think you were?'

'I . . . I wasn't sure.'

'Where've you come from then?'

'South . . . London way . . .' she murmured vaguely.

'You should have taken the M4 or M40.'

'I . . . I don't like motorways.'

'So where in Wales are you heading then?'

'West . . . near Aberystwyth.'

He let out a low whistle. 'Come out of your way a bit, haven't you? Best thing you can do is go back to Brecon, and then take the A40 through Sennybridge to Llandovery, pick up the A482 to Lampeter, and then—'

'It's all right. I know my way from there.'

'Live that way, do you?'

'My parents do . . . I'm on my way to see them.'

She slid behind the wheel, slammed her car door, and raised a hand in farewell as she drove off the forecourt.

As she turned right he came limping after her, waving his arms, shouting, 'That's the wrong way! You're going towards Builth Wells!'

Now that she had a tank full of petrol, Maureen Flynn's confidence returned. She smiled to herself as she saw the garage man standing in the road waving his arms. She wasn't heading for Aberystwyth, but if he wanted to think she was then that was all to the good.

She didn't know why she had said she was visiting her parents. That hadn't been her intention, but since she was in Wales she might as well head north and do exactly that.

It was only about a hundred miles from Builth Wells to Llangollen, and the roads were quiet at this time of the year, especially at night. She'd be there in a couple of hours or so, but she must stop first and get rid of the black plastic bag, she reminded herself. She grimaced as she thought of the shock her father would get if he came out to the car to help carry in her cases and picked that up by mistake.

But she didn't have any luggage! How on earth was she going to explain that to them?

She blanked it from her mind. She'd think of something. They'd probably be so surprised to see her that they'd swallow any story, she told herself. The important thing now was to get rid of the black bin bag.

As she drove along the almost deserted roads, with their wide verges, clumps of trees and dense hedges, she was very tempted to toss it down into one of the deep ditches. That would get rid of it, but it might be risky. Storing up trouble for later on if someone came along and found it and opened it up. Not that they would be able to link it to her, of course! She'd been far too clever to leave any clues.

Even so, she decided, she'd stick to her original plan. She'd dispose of it in a household rubbish tip. That had proved a very successful way of doing things all along, so why change the routine now? She'd drive round the next town she came to until she found one. They were usually on the outskirts and clearly signposted.

She drew a blank a both Newton and Welshpool, and as she circled the periphery of each of the towns she found she was losing her sense of direction.

A sense of bewilderment clouded her mind. It was now quite dark so she could hardly stop and ask directions to the local household waste tip without attracting attention. Another thirty miles and she'd be in Llangollen. She had to find somewhere to get rid of the bag before then, and the only large town was Oswestry.

She felt desperately hungry, so she consoled herself with the promise that she'd definitely stop at Oswestry for food and a drink. A place that size *must* have a household waste depot of some kind she told herself, trying to quell the panic rising inside her.

Perhaps she wouldn't bother about a drink or anything to eat. Disposing of the black plastic bag before she started on the final leg of her journey to Llangollen was the top priority. Her mother would give her all the food and drink she wanted once she reached there.

Simon Gould checked the time on his wrist watch and saw that it had turned eight o'clock. He might as well close up for the night, he decided. Maggie would have his supper ready by now. Anyway, he felt too tired to work on the Citroën that had come in for repairs. He'd start on it first thing in the morning.

As he kicked off his boots by the back door, and washed his hands at the kitchen sink, he wondered how far his last customer had got before she realized she was going in the wrong direction and turned back.

It wasn't until he and Maggie had eaten the cottage pie followed by apple tart and custard that she'd cooked for their evening meal, and they were sitting over a pot of tea, that he told her about it.

'The funny thing is,' he mused, 'I thought I knew her. I'm sure I've seen her somewhere before, but I can't quite place her.'

'If she wasn't one of the locals then she might be one of them townies that have the summer cottages and only comes here once or twice a year,' Maggie suggested.

He shook his head. 'I don't think so.'

'It does happen,' she persisted. 'I've met one of them before now down at the shop, and for the life of me I can't put a name to the face. Then it comes back to me. One of them summer cottage people.'

'She sounded as though she'd come from London way . . .'

'There you are then!' Maggie smiled triumphantly. 'Like I said. One of the summer people.' She frowned. 'Rotten lot they are. Coming here, and buying up the cottages that the young couples should be making their homes in.'

Simon laughed. 'Cut it out! You know full well that the youngsters round here can't wait to get away from the place. Down to Cardiff, or Bristol, the moment they leave school.'

'Not all of them. Look at Betti Jenkins . . .'

'She only stayed on here because she'd got a baby to bring up.'

'Yeah! And I wouldn't mind betting that the father of that child was one of these summer people!' Maggie added darkly.

'You and your summer people! We'd have no trade if it wasn't for them. Look how slack things are at the moment.'

She looked at him balefully. 'They're strangers. They don't belong around here.'

'Neither do I,' he teased. 'D'ye want me to up and leave?'

'Oh, go on with you. You know what I mean. Anyway, you were the one who started all this talk about strangers.'

'I only said that I thought I knew this woman from some-where. She seemed to be in a right dream,' he went on. 'She asked where the nearest town was, and when I told her Brecon was in one direction, and Builth Wells in the other, she seemed surprised to learn she was in Wales.'

'Then she wouldn't be one of the summer people if she'd never been here before.'

'No, I agree with that. But she had been to Wales before. She said her folks lived Aberystwyth way.'

'Then you couldn't have met her before, because neither of us knows anyone who lives at Aberystwyth, now do we?'

'Maybe I knew her when I lived down near London.'

Maggie gave an exaggerated sigh. 'You do say some daft things. I sometimes think that bang on the head you got left you puddled.'

'You never know, she might have been an old flame come looking for me,' he joked.

'And when she found you she didn't like the look of you, and so she drove off in such a hurry that she went the wrong way,' chortled Maggie.

'Well, that's all right then, isn't it?' He laughed and pulled her into his arms. 'You wouldn't want some other woman coming along and taking me away from you, now, would you?'

'Chance would be a find thing,' she bantered, but her response to his embrace left him in no doubt about her feelings.

He sighed as he buried his face in her curly dark hair. He'd been lucky finding someone like Maggie. Not many girls would have wanted to be seen with him after his car crash, he'd ended up so crippled and disfigured.

Maggie had been the nurse assigned to sit by his bed all through the long hours when he'd been in a critical condition in intensive care. She'd help him pull through, and when he'd been moved off the danger list, and into an ordinary ward, she'd visited him daily, often in her off-duty hours.

If it hadn't been for her gentle banter and fierce insistence on him getting better, he'd never have survived the painful skin grafts or the months of physiotherapy before he could walk again. She'd been nurse, mother, teacher and then, after he'd been discharged from hospital, his lover.

The weeks of sheer bliss became mental anguish when he knew that he couldn't live without her. It had taken tremendous courage to propose because he'd been afraid that asking her to marry him might break the spell.

But it hadn't. Maggie had given up nursing, insisting that they'd be happier living in the country than in a town.

'We'll find a village like the one where I grew up,' she told him. 'After a few months people will accept you, and you'll forget about your limp.'

'But not about my face!' His fingers traced the livid scars

that ran from the corner of his left eye down to his chin, a permanent memento of his crash.

'Three months and no one will see that,' she promised.

'How do you make that out?'

'Grow a beard!'

He'd taken her advice. It had taken longer than three months, but once it was established, dark and thick, covering his cheeks and chin, the scar was almost invisible.

There had been one other stroke of good fortune. The manufacturers of the car he'd been driving when the accident had happened desperately wanted to hush up the fact that the car had been faulty. Their compensation was extremely generous.

Knowing how much he loved cars, and realizing that he would never be able to race again, Maggie had suggested they should invest the money in a garage. 'My uncle has a garage in Pontydaren, not far from Brecon,' she told him. 'He's talking about retiring soon. Why not go and work with him for a few months and see if you like the idea of running a garage? If you do, then you could buy it off him.'

Like all Maggie's suggestions it had been a winner. Four months later her uncle had moved out of the garage into a small cottage in the village, and Simon and Maggie had moved into the three-bedroom bungalow that adjoined the garage.

That had been almost ten years ago, Simon reflected. What had been little more than a filling station selling spares, now had its own repair bays and car wash and kept him busy from first thing in the morning until dusk.

Being on the main road from Brecon to Builth Wells there was plenty of passing trade during the summer months, and even in winter there was enough repair work, as well as the odd passer-by dropping in for fuel, to keep him going. Like the woman this evening, the one he was sure he knew from somewhere.

'Well, she certainly didn't recognize you or she'd have said so,' Maggie pointed out when he brought the subject up again as they were undressing for bed.

It wasn't until after they'd put the lights out, that Simon remembered.

'I was at school with her,' he exclaimed, startling Maggie.

'What are you on about?' she mumbled sleepily, pulling the duvet up over her ears.

'That woman I was telling you about, the one who came for petrol just before I closed tonight. I was at school with her in Benbury. I can't remember what her name was. Mary . . . Mandy . . . Something like that. We were in the Upper Sixth . . . She was the only girl in our year who passed her A-levels. Maureen! That was her name. I remember it now. Maureen . . . Maureen Flynn.'

TWENTY-ONE

D avy Howells prided himself on having the best kept household waste disposal tip in Wales . . . or in Great Britain for that matter. Two years running, LLansilin had won the Municipal Environment Award. And he intended it should do so again this year. Three awards in as many years! A hat trick!

This year he was planning a garden theme. He was going to build a patio outside his caravan using all the broken stone slabs that were lying around the place. Then he'd arrange flower boxes, and conifers in tubs, around the edges and various garden ornaments and gnomes standing between them. He might even put out one or two of the garden tables and plastic chairs he'd rescued from the skips and stacked up behind his caravan. None of them matched, but if he fixed up a couple of the garden umbrellas he'd salvaged it would look quite continental.

Living on the site, like he did, he took a pride in making his surroundings look attractive. And he made sure that no one ruined his efforts by dumping bags of rubbish anywhere except in the appropriate skip!

Nothing annoyed Davy more than when someone put glass in with paper, or rags in the skip marked 'Metal Only'. He labelled them all clearly enough, It was sheer carelessness. Lack of respect because it was a rubbish tip.

Such people totally ignored his hard work in trying to keep the place looking clean and attractive, and he hated them for it. It took him all his time not to show it. One of these days when someone messed up his lovely clean paths after he'd swept them, or dumped rubbish in the wrong skip, he knew he would thump them!

What roused him even more than all these things was when people arrived late, found he had locked the six foot high iron gates, and left their bags of rubbish outside it. More often than not, before he found them next morning, the foxes, or stray dogs, would scratch a great hole in the side of the bag, spilling the contents all over the roadway in front of the gate.

The very next time that happened he intended calling the police. He wasn't quite sure what sort of charge it would be, but he was sure he'd be able to think of one if they could trace the person who'd left the bag.

The double iron gates of the Llansilin household waste site were not simply closed but securely locked when Maureen Flynn drew up outside.

She felt incensed. Fancy locking the gates! Who on earth would want to steal anything from a rubbish tip, she thought angrily as she rattled them to make sure they really were locked.

Now what was she to do, she wondered. She didn't want to turn up at her parents' house with the black plastic bag still in the boot of her car, yet she daren't leave it propped up against the gates in case a fox, or some other animal, ripped it open before morning.

It was a pity one of the skips wasn't near enough for her to toss the bag straight in. The only alternative was to toss the bag over and rely on the fact that whoever unlocked the gate in the morning and found it lying there would dump it into the skip.

No, that was too risky, she decided. She was about to turn away when she saw there was a light shining in the caravan parked just inside the gates, and through the uncurtained window she could see a man moving about inside the caravan. Maureen rattled the iron gates as noisily as she could, hoping to attract his attention.

In the stillness that bathed Llansilin the noise was deafening. The man paused in what he was doing, peered out of the window, and to her relief came out of the caravan. He didn't come over to the gates, but stood on the pathway waving at her to go away.

'We're closed! Come back in the morning.'

'I can't do that,' she yelled back. 'I have to go to work.'

Grumbling, he walked over to the gates and unbolted them.

He may as well take the stuff in as have to pick it up from the path in the morning, he thought. At least she hadn't just left the bags and cleared off. 'Give it here!'

'No, I'll put it in the skip myself,' she told him.

'Oh no! I'm not letting anyone past these gates once they're locked for the night,' he told her stubbornly, and he grabbed at the black plastic bag she was holding.

For a split second they stood there glaring at each other, neither prepared to relinquish their hold on the bag. With a sudden jerk, he pulled it from her, and he immediately slammed the iron gates and began bolting them from his side.

Knowing there was nothing she could do, Maureen backed away. 'Thanks!' she shouted over her shoulder as she reached her car.

Now that the bag was gone she felt an overwhelming sense of relief. She began to wonder why on earth she had got so worked up and come all this way simply to get away from Benbury.

She drove on in a daze, wondering if she had panicked over nothing. When the signposts indicated that she had only about another five miles to go she was filled with misgivings as to whether she was doing the right thing in visiting her parents. They were bound to ask questions about why she was there, and why she hadn't let them know in advance that she was coming.

Perhaps she should turn round and go back to Benbury!

She'd disposed of the evidence, and there was no way anyone could ever link anything in the black plastic bag to her, so what was she worrying about? All along she'd been incredibly careful never to leave a single clue so that there was nothing at all that could be traced to her.

She'd achieved what she'd set out to do. All four of the boys who'd raped her when she'd been eighteen were now dead, and the police didn't have the slightest indication who might have killed them.

Even though there wasn't the remotest reason why they should connect her with the crime, it might be better if she went back to Dutton, however, and lived as she normally did. She didn't know many people, but her neighbours were probably aware of her routine, even if she didn't study theirs.

Still undecided about what to do, she decided to stop at the next pub she came to and have a drink. A celebration all on her own, she told herself as she pulled into the car park of the Golden Lamb. And while she was having it she'd make her mind up about whether to go back to Dutton or carry on and visit her parents.

A log fire was blazing in the lounge bar, but the customers were all in the public bar, engrossed in a game of darts. The barman broke away just long enough to serve her with a drink.

Maureen took her glass of vodka and tonic over to one of the tables near the fire. Warm and comfortable, she sat there sipping her drink and relaxed. The background noises of the darts game, and the television suspended on a bracket over the bar, lulled her senses so that she could easily have drifted off to sleep.

Suddenly, she was wide awake. The news programme was on, and the announcer was giving details of Dennis Jackson's murder.

'The police are anxious to trace a man and a woman who may be able to help them with their enquiries.'

She stared in horror as two photographs were flashed on to the screen.

'They are Maureen Flynn and Simon Gould,' went on the crisp tones of the announcer. 'These pictures were taken a number of years ago. Photofit experts state these two people could now look like this.'

Two more faces appeared, artists impressions of what the two people might possible look sixteen years later.

When Maureen saw the one of herself she almost laughed aloud with relief. It bore no resemblance to what she looked like. In the photofit her hair was shoulder length, and she looked plump-faced and motherly.

She drained her glass and left. There was no question of visiting her parents now. They had probably seen the news, and they would be bound to recognize the photo taken when she was eighteen. They might remember Dennis Jackson's name, too! She hadn't thought of that. He was the only one whose name they would remember. She wasn't even sure if she had told them the names of the other boys who'd been involved.

No, she must get right away. But where? No one in Dutton knew she had once lived in Benbury. And they certainly wouldn't recognize her from those pictures on TV, so it might be best to go back to her flat and simply act as though nothing had happened. She could lie low until all the hullabaloo about the murders died down.

Or she could pack some clothes, clear everything out of the flat and simply disappear. She could go abroad! She had enough money saved up to live on for a few months. Take a train to France then start a new life. Researchers were always wanted in EEC countries.

If she didn't like living in Europe she could always come home again. Not back to Benbury, of course. London would be safe though. Or Dublin. She quite fancied living in Ireland. America might be a safer place to hide. But she'd need a work permit if she went there!

Her mind was a seething whirlpool of confusion. She couldn't decide what to do for the best. Except to head back south. Return to her flat and act as if nothing had happened.

There wasn't a shred of evidence to connect her with the murders, she reminded herself. She was positive about that.

Even if the police did trace her from that photograph, it wouldn't really matter. She'd have to admit she had known Moorhouse, and Franklin, and all the others when she'd been at school, but she could say that she'd never seen any of them again after she'd left Benbury. No one, except her parents, had any idea why she'd left, and they had been so ashamed by what happened that they were hardly likely to tell anyone now.

No, she was quite safe, absolutely in the clear, as long as she kept her nerve and acted normally.

'D'ye mean to tell me, boyo, that you've dragged us all the way out here simply to tell us that someone tossed a black bag full of rubbish over the gates last night after you were closed?'

'No, no, no! Of course not,' Davy Howells exclaimed

indignantly. 'If I called you out every time some inconsiderate person did that then you'd be living on my doorstep.'

'So what is the problem?'

'This bin bag, see. Brought to the gate after I'd closed last night—'

'I thought you said that wasn't the reason,' Sergeant Thomas interrupted sharply. 'Look, Howells, I told you . . .'

'Hold on, hold on, Sarge. Hear me out, man!'

'Go on, then.'

'Well, it's not the bag, see. Like I told you, they're always tossing them over the gate, or leaving them on the path outside. This one is different. A woman came with it, and she stood there rattling the gate until I came out, see!'

Sergeant Thomas's face hardened. 'So?'

'It's what's inside it, see!'

'So what is inside it . . . A body?'

The sergeant laughed at his own joke, then stopped when he saw the uneasy look on Davy Howells' face. 'It's not a body, is it?'

'Not exactly. I think it might have something to do with a body though.'

'What do you mean?' The banter had gone from Sergeant Thomas's voice. Now it was sharp, questioning.

'Look for yourself.' Davy Howells opened the neck of the black plastic bag and upended it, tipping the contents on to the ground in front of them. 'See what I mean!' Davy pointed to the miscellany of clothes and the pair of trainers. 'They're all brand new!' He bent down to pick up one of the trainers. 'Perfect, except for a dark stain on the toe of one of them.'

'Don't touch it!' Sergeant Thomas pushed him away. 'We don't want your fingerprints on them,' he added by way of explanation.

'I've already handled them,' Davy told him. 'I checked over what was in the bag before I phoned you, see.'

The sergeant looked at him quizzically, waiting for him to go on.

'Anything left at this site is mine; that's part of the agreement I have with the council,' Davy Howells told him defensively. 'As a rule, mind, I don't bother looking into bags that are tied up. Usually they're only a lot of rubbish, see! This was different. I took it off the woman. Then when I was tossing it up into the skip the bag split open. I spotted the pair of black tracksuit bottoms, and those trainers, and they looked new, so I thought I'd see if they fitted me. Then I saw that mark on the trainers . . .' He paused and shuddered. 'Never could stand the sight of blood . . .'

'So you phoned the station.'

Davy Howells nodded. 'I did the right thing, didn't I, Sergeant?'

'Yes, you did, Davy. You'd better come down to the station later on so that we can take your prints, and you can give us a description of the person who handed you the bag.'

Davy gave him a crafty look. 'Does that mean there might be some kind of reward?'

Sergeant Thomas pulled on his driving gloves, picked up the plastic sack, and started to walk away. 'Thanks for your trouble.'

'Hold on! Don't I get a receipt or anything?'

'What for? You said yourself it was only rubbish!'

'I want compensation! I could have worn those clothes and the trainers.'

Sergeant Thomas grinned as he loaded the bag into the boot of his panda car. 'Nice try, Davy, but I'm afraid it won't work. Don't forget to pop into the station,' he added as he started up his car. 'Otherwise you might find someone calling on you with a pair of handcuffs!'

TWENTY-TWO

'**S**uperintendent Wilson wants us in his office right away!'
The look Detective Inspector Ruth Morgan exchanged
with Detective Sergeant Paddy Hardcastle conveyed
more than any words could have done. It also emphasized
the camaraderie that had slowly developed between them
while they had been working on the Benbury murders, and
the way they had both changed their opinion of each other.

When he had first been assigned as her sergeant, Paddy had
resented the fact that she had been appointed inspector over
his head. He was the one with experience, whereas she had
gone straight from university to police training college with
no practical knowledge whatsoever. He'd soon discovered,
however, that she was dedicated to the job, and though she
thought differently to him, the way she reasoned things out
was stimulating and kept him on his toes.

For her part, Ruth had discovered that Paddy was not just a
handsome six-footer with broad shoulders and a bland expression. Beneath that bluff exterior was a brain honed by experience
that complimented her own shrewd reasoning.

Their early days had been marred by their suspicion of each
other. Once they had discovered that working in tandem was
preferable to each of them trying to score points, they became
a formidable team.

They were still not sure that Detective Superintendent
Wilson realized this, however. At every meeting he called
he had indicated that he was still not satisfied with the
progress they were making on the Benbury Murders. Some
of the victims had been fellow members of his Masonic
lodge, which accounted for the keen interest he was taking
in the case.

'If it is the work of a serial killer then perhaps he thinks
his name is on the hit list as well,' Paddy said with a grimace.

'Come on.' Ruth gathered up her notes. 'Let's get it over.

Our news this morning should convince him that we are making progress at last.'

Superintendent Wilson listened impassively as Ruth gave him details of their latest piece of evidence.

'Have each of the items been checked out by Forensic yet?'

'Yes, sir. And the stains on the trainers are the same blood group as Dennis Jackson's.'

'And they were found near Oswestry, you say?'

'That's correct, sir. The caretaker of a household waste site at Llansilin notified his local police. They were in a black plastic bin bag that had been handed in by a woman after he had closed last night,' she affirmed.

'The logo on the instep of the trainer also ties in with the print found at the scene of Brian Patterson's murder,' added Paddy.

'Have you checked out where the trainers were bought?'

'Not yet, sir. It's next on our list.'

Superintendent Jackson scowled. 'And what about the two people in the photograph. Any sightings?'

'No, sir. The trouble is those photographs are almost twenty years old. Both the man and the woman will have changed since then and—'

'Someone should recognize them. Friends from those days.' He turned to Paddy. 'Didn't you say the man, Simon Gould, had gone into the car business?'

'That was what Mr Perks, the history teacher from Benbury Secondary School, thought. Gould was a racing driver for a time. Then he met with a very bad accident and—'

'Have you contacted all the petrol companies to see if any of them supply a garage run by a chap of that name?' interrupted the inspector impatiently.

'It's being done now, sir,' Ruth told him. 'As soon as we get a lead we'll investigate further.'

'When you do, I want one of you visit the garage yourself, interview the fellow, find out what he knows. Understand?'

'Of course, sir.'

'It's more than likely that he's our man.'

'Sir?' Ruth looked puzzled.

'Have you forgotten everything you learned at training college about serial killers, Inspector?'

'No! Of course not, but—'

'Then surely you can see that he has a motive. A man who had a promising future until he met with an accident; a man so badly scarred that he's retreated from all his friends to start a new life. A man who probably sustained head injuries that have changed his entire personality and who now has a grudge against life, especially against his boyhood contemporaries who have all done well for themselves.'

'There was also a girl in that school group,' Ruth said stubbornly.

'Yes! What was her name?'

'Maureen Flynn.'

'Have you anything else on her?'

'She was the only girl at Benbury Secondary School who passed her A-levels that year. She and her family left Benbury soon afterwards.'

'Find her. She may be in grave danger if this fellow Gould is our man!'

'Or she might be the killer,' Ruth observed, then bit her lip as she saw the look of anger mingled with surprise on the superintendent's face.

His eyes were hooded as he stared hard at her. 'You mean you're looking for a woman?'

'The trainer imprint was quite a small size. More likely to belong to a woman than a man.'

'And the black jeans?'

She hesitated. 'Unisex. They could have been worn by a man or a woman.'

'And why would a woman want to kill four men who had been at school with her?'

Ruth shook her head. 'I don't know.'

'And what do you think, Sergeant? Do you think it might have been a woman?'

Paddy felt uncomfortable. There was a sneer in the superintendent's voice, and he suspected that Wilson intended him to ridicule Ruth's theory. Desperately, he tried to think of some way of supporting his colleague. 'The men were all stabbed,' he hazarded. 'Statistics show that a man is more likely to shoot his victim.'

'So you both think this woman suddenly decides to kill all the men she was at school with almost twenty years ago?'

'It's possible . . .'

'Why?' The thunder of the superintendent's voice silenced Paddy. 'Come on. If that is what you think, why do you think it?'

Paddy looked flummoxed. He shot a glance at Ruth, a silent plea for help, but before she could intervene, Superintendent Wilson stood up, indicating that the interview was at an end.

'I want Simon Gould and Maureen Flynn found without delay,' he barked. 'Fetch both of them in for questioning. Do you understand? Oh, and one more thing,' he stated as they were about to leave his office. 'Don't forget to find out where those trainers were bought!'

Tracing the shops which stocked the trainers proved surprisingly easy. They were a special consignment that had been imported from Korea, and the logo was an exclusive trademark.

The importers supplied a small chain of shops called Quicksale and were able to provide a list of all their shops which had taken a delivery of the trainers. None of them were in Benbury.

'The nearest seems to be in Dutton, about fifty miles away,' mused Paddy. 'Shall I go and check it out?'

'No, I will. You try and locate this fellow Gould,' Ruth told him.

They still had some of the trainers in stock at Dutton, and the manager confirmed that usually they were purchased by women customers.

'They're not broad enough for most boys or young men,' he explained.

They'd sold about a dozen pairs in varying sizes. Two of the pairs sold could possibly have provided the imprint found at the scene of Brian Patterson's murder.

'You do keep a record of each sale?' Ruth asked, hopefully.

'Not the name of the customer, I'm afraid.' He shrugged. 'All they want is a receipt to check against their credit card statement . . .'

'But you do have a record of their credit card number?'

He frowned, as if unable to see where her question was leading.

'If you have the customer's credit card number then the credit card company will have a record of the customer's name,' she pointed out. 'Can you turn them up for me?'

Ten minutes later she had the good news . . . and the bad. One pair of trainers had been bought by credit card, but that transaction had only taken place the previous day. The other pair had been bought a few days before Patterson's murder, but the customer had paid in cash.

'Can we ask the assistant who made the sale if she remembers anything about the customer?' Ruth pressed.

'We can ask her.'

The assistant was a smart, pleasant-faced girl in her early twenties. 'Yes, I remember the sale,' she told them brightly. 'They were bought by a slim dark woman in her mid-thirties. I thought it rather odd that someone as smartly dressed as she was should be buying trainers. Then I thought that perhaps she went jogging to keep fit.'

Ruth smiled. 'That is most helpful. Do you always remember your customers in such detail?'

The girl shook her head. 'No! I remember this customer because I was working as a holiday relief at our Endover shop a couple of days later, and she came in there and bought another pair of identical trainers!'

'You served her?'

'No. The girl who did passed the same comment though – that she didn't look the sort of person to buy trainers . . . Not cheap ones, anyway.'

'So, how well can you describe her?'

'Well, like I said, she was slim and wearing a suit. Nothing flashy; bit drab, in fact.

'Anything else?'

'Not much make-up. She was pleasant but quite ordinary looking, really.'

'And her voice?'

The girl shrugged. 'She didn't speak. Except to say "thank you" when I handed over her change.'

'She must have told you what size trainer she wanted.'

'No.' The girl shook her head. 'All our stock there is laid out so that customers can make their own selection. They are left to browse and try the shoes on. When they find what they want they bring them over to the counter and pay for them.'

'You don't talk to them . . .? Try to sell them something else?'

She shrugged. 'That's usually a waste of time. Most of them resent it if you suggest they even look at anything else. They know what they want before they come in. If we've got it they buy it, and if we haven't they go to another shop.'

Sergeant Hardcastle had almost come to the conclusion that they had been misinformed about Simon Gould being in the motor trade. None of the larger petrol companies had anyone of that name on their books.

'We have no tenant or manager of that name. He probably has his own garage and trades under a company name,' he was told over and over again.

'Have you tried Swansea? If he does MOTs then he might be on their records,' suggested Ruth. 'I still think it's a waste of time chasing after him,' she added.

She had already told Paddy how successful she'd been in tracing the trainers. He'd agreed with her that buying two pairs within as many days was highly suspicious. It had been a long shot, but since the first pair of trainers had been bought in Dutton, Ruth had gone through the local electoral list to see if there was a Maureen Flynn living in the town. And it had paid off. A Maureen Flynn lived at Twenty-Five Windermere Mews.

'We'll go and have a word with her,' stated Ruth. 'If she's the person we're looking for there mightn't be any need to trace Simon Gould.'

They were on the outskirts of Dutton before Paddy asked the question that had been troubling him for the past hour.

'Why are you so certain that the killer is a woman? Apart from the theory I put forward to the inspector's office that men don't usually stab their victims, that is.'

She was silent for such a long time that he shot a sideways glance to see if she had heard his question.

'Intuition.'

He took another swift glance to see if she was laughing at him, but her face was patterned by the changing light and the shadows from the trees that lined the road they were driving along.

'I don't understand.'

'It was that photograph that set me thinking. The only girl in that year who had proved that she was as good as the boys. And then she completely disappears! No one in Benbury seems to know what happened to her afterwards . . . not even her teachers or the boys she had been at school with and who were in the photograph with her.'

'Mr Perks said that she and her family left Benbury.'

'Yes, I know but why did they leave Benbury and where did they move to? She obviously didn't go on to university or there would be something in her school records.'

'Obviously she moved to Dutton . . .'

'Did she! Is this the Maureen Flynn we are looking for, or is it someone with the same name? She would be in her mid-thirties by now, remember, and it's more than likely she would be married and have changed her name.'

He nodded. 'True. So why are we chasing after this Maureen Flynn, then?'

Ruth was silent for a moment. 'I don't think she did marry. I think that perhaps she was in love with one of those boys in the photograph, perhaps with more than one of them, and something went wrong.'

'So you think that this is some sort of revenge killing?'

'Something like that. They all married and had families.'

'Sandy Franklin wasn't married.'

'Maybe she thought he was since he lived over his shop.'

Paddy wasn't convinced. 'I think that puts paid to your theory that it was some form of revenge because they married and she didn't,' he said firmly.

'Maybe it does,' Ruth admitted reluctantly. 'I still think the killings have something to do with what happened when they were all at school. There's a link, if only we can find it.'

'Most of the links we've established between them don't appear to mean a thing,' he pointed out. 'We know they were the same age, at school together and passed their A-levels in the same year. None of them seem to have any financial problems, or criminal records of any kind, apart from one minor driving offence. They obviously stayed on good terms with each other since Patterson acted as solicitor for both Franklin and Jackson—'

'And we know that both Franklin and Patterson belonged to the same Masonic lodge as Superintendent Wilson,' interrupted Ruth.

'Which means the only two we have no details about are Gould and the woman. You know –' he shot her another glance – 'we might have done better to concentrate on tracing Gould.'

'We're in Dutton now so we may as well talk to Maureen Flynn . . . if only to give you and the superintendent the satisfaction of being able to eliminate her from our list of suspects,' said Ruth stubbornly.

TWENTY-THREE

'Let's hope the enquiries we put in motion before we set out for Dutton have brought in more satisfactory results than the ones we've managed to achieve,' groaned Ruth Morgan as they drove back to Benbury from Dutton. 'It's been a complete waste of our time.'

'Not a complete waste,' said Paddy with a grin. 'The neighbours were quite helpful.'

'I suppose we should have got a search warrant before we left.'

'We weren't even sure that it was the right person . . .'

'No and we still aren't,' Ruth muttered moodily.

'We would have had to force an entry . . .'

Ruth didn't answer. Her thoughts were in turmoil. She'd followed a hunch and drawn a blank, and it irritated her. She was still sure in her own mind that Maureen Flynn was the one responsible for the multiple murders in Benbury, but from the information they had gleaned from Maureen Flynn's neighbours it was impossible to decide whether she was right or not.

What she needed was proof: proof that was so sound that she could present it to Superintendent Wilson without a qualm.

'Shall we stop for a coffee before we go back to the station? There's a Little Chef about a mile up the road,' suggested Paddy, breaking into her reverie.

'No, Sergeant. We've already wasted enough time this afternoon on an abortive investigation,' she snapped.

From out of the corner of her eye she saw his face freeze and his knuckles whiten as he tightened his grip on the wheel.

She bit her lip. It wasn't his fault that the trip had been fruitless. He obviously knew she was uptight, and probably his intention had been to help her unwind before facing Superintendent Wilson.

She laid a hand on his arm. 'Sorry, Paddy. No point taking

my frustrations out on you. Yes, we'll stop. As long as it's my shout.' She smiled to herself, knowing he was about to argue on that point, so as they drew up outside the Little Chef, she handed him a ten-pound note.

He hesitated for a moment, then with a resigned shrug took the money from her.

Ruth found that the hot coffee not only helped her to calm down, but helped to clear the jumble inside her head.

'I think we'd better concentrate on Simon Gould,' she admitted, after they'd gone over the few details they had been able to extract from Maureen Flynn's neighbours.

'It's a pity none of them knew where her parents live.'

'One of the women was pretty sure it was Wales . . . and that that was where she'd gone,' Ruth said.

'Mmm! But she didn't know which part of Wales.'

'Quite! And it's a fair sized country.'

'Or she could be working away from home,' Paddy suggested.

'True!'

'One woman did say that she understood she worked as a freelance researcher, and that occasionally she did go away on business.'

'If we can't locate her then it's impossible to warn her that she might possibly be in danger.'

'Which certainly won't please the superintendent.'

'The only way to placate him is by finding Simon Gould before he finds Maureen Flynn.'

'Or before she finds him . . .'

They stared at each other, appalled by their own thoughts.

A batch of faxes were waiting for Detective Inspector Ruth Morgan when she and Detective Sergeant Paddy Hardcastle arrived back at Benbury Police station.

A man called Simon Gould had been located, but whether or not he was the right man had yet to be established, although it seemed more than likely that he was.

'Runs a garage in Pontydaren, wherever that might be,' murmured Paddy as she handed him the fax.

'It's in Wales. In South Wales, to be exact, just north of

Brecon on the road to Builth Wells. It's an area I know quite well . . .'

'Wales? Maureen Flynn is believed to have gone to Wales . . .'

Their gaze locked.

'Let's go,' ordered Ruth. 'I'll read the rest of these on the way,' she added as she gathered up the batch of papers from her desk.

The Pontydaren Garage was still open when Detective Inspector Ruth Morgan and Detective Sergeant Paddy Hardcastle drove on to the forecourt.

They watched the man who emerged from the repair shop at the rear limp over to them. A rangy figure, he had a heavy black beard that almost covered his face, making it impossible to tell whether he was thirty, forty or fifty.

'Petrol?'

'Are you Simon Gould?'

The man stiffened. 'Could be. Who's asking?'

'I'm DS Hardcastle and this is DI Morgan.' Paddy pulled out his warrant card to establish his identity. 'We'd like a word with you.'

'Oh yes! What about?'

'Could we go inside? It might take some time.'

The man hesitated, then shrugged. 'Could you move your car away from the pumps first?'

'Of course!'

Paddy restarted the engine and parked where Simon Gould indicated. Ruth picked up her briefcase and accompanied both men towards a bungalow at the side of the garage forecourt.

'Come in,' he invited, and stood aside to allow them to enter. 'Maggie! We've got visitors!'

His shout brought a plump dark-haired woman hurrying from the kitchen area.

'Police,' he said laconically. 'We'll be in the sitting room. Listen out for the forecourt bell, will you? Oh, and I bet a cup of tea wouldn't go amiss.' He looked enquiringly at Ruth and Paddy.

'Now,' he said, when they were seated. 'What can I do for you?'

'We hope you can help us with our enquiries,' Paddy told him.

Before they even began to talk to him, Ruth was quite sure that if this man was the Simon Gould they were looking for then he wasn't their murderer. Not unless he was a very good actor.

Their arrival hadn't caused him the slightest sign of distress, only a modicum of irritation at being taken away from whatever it was he was doing in his workshop. She felt confident that her own theory was the right one. It was Maureen Flynn they should be looking for, not this man.

Still, it mightn't be a completely wasted journey, she consoled herself. If he was the right Simon Gould then he might be able to help. And he was alive, which was more than the others were.

'We're investigating the Benbury murders—'

Simon Gould frowned. 'Did you say Benbury? I used to live there when I was younger,' he interrupted. 'I went to school there, as a matter of fact.'

'We thought that might be so, Mr Gould. That's why we're here.'

'What about it?' He looked at them in surprise. 'Did you say something about murders?'

'You mean you haven't read about the four Benbury men who have been killed recently?' exclaimed Ruth.

He shook his head. 'I hardly ever have time to look at newspapers.'

'There have been reports on the radio and TV most nights . . .'

'I never watch the box. Maggie, the wife, does. She loves watching all the soaps. It can be pretty lonely stuck out here, you see, especially during the winter months. They've become her life. She'd watch them all day given the chance. But the news?' He laughed. 'We don't bother with that. She says its nothing but bad news, and it gets her down hearing about all those wars and seeing women and kids being blown up.'

Ruth felt more convinced than ever that he wasn't the person responsible for the murders. 'You probably recognize everyone on this,' she commented as she produced the school photograph and held it out to him.

He studied it for a moment, rubbing a hand over his beard. 'Now there's a coincidence!' He jabbed at the picture of Maureen Flynn. 'I thought I saw her just a couple of days ago . . .'

'You did? Where?'

'Right here! She pulled in for petrol. I was sure it was her.'

'Did she recognize you?'

Simon Gould laughed. 'Looking like I do now! Would you have recognized me if you hadn't seen me since I was a fresh-faced young schoolboy?'

'Yet you recognized her?'

He nodded. 'I was pretty sure it was her, though it's over fifteen years since I last saw her and that picture was taken . . .' He paused and pulled thoughtfully at his beard. 'I was pretty sure it was her. I said so to Maggie when I came indoors. She never knew her, of course.'

'And you say you haven't seen or heard of Maureen Flynn since that picture was taken?'

'No. Why should I have? I never had very much to do with her when we were at school. Or with any of those boys either. It was only because we were the ones who'd passed our A-levels that we were in that picture together.'

'A ritual form of celebration,' observed Ruth.

'So the head thought! We had other ideas about how to celebrate.' He laughed again, as if reliving the memory.

'So, how did you celebrate?'

'Down to the pub, of course! Drinks all round. It seemed big at the time, but I had no stomach for beer. Two beers and I was outside spewing my guts up. The others left me there . . .' He paused, as if reluctant to say any more.

'Go on. What happened afterwards?' pressed Paddy.

'I'm not too sure. The other four, and the girl, went off towards the Mire. It had once been allotments, but no one bothered with it any more. It was just derelict ground with an old shed standing in the middle of it.'

'And you didn't go with them?'

'No. Like I said, I was still spewing up.'

'So how do you know that's where they went?'

'They bragged about it next day. Kept hinting about how I'd missed out.'

'What had you missed out on?' pursued Ruth.

He looked at her in astonishment. 'There were four of them and only the one girl! Think about it. We were eighteen, and we'd just heard we'd passed our exams after two years of nose-to-the-grindstone studying. They were ecstatic! Looking for ways of letting off steam . . .'

'You mean a sex orgy?'

'Sex orgy. Gang-bang. Call it what you will . . .'

'Which you had no part in?'

He shook his head. 'I told you, I was feeling too groggy to go with them. I could hardly stand up!'

'So how do you know that this is what happened?'

'John Moorhouse called round the next day to see if I was alright. He said he felt bad about clearing off and leaving me, because of the state I was in.'

'And he told you what happened?'

Simon Gould nodded. 'Yes. I think he was feeling pretty bad about it.'

'In what way?' Do you mean they forced her to take part? Or, in other words, they raped her?'

Simon Gould shrugged. 'John Moorhouse was a nice bloke. Quiet type. He had a steady girlfriend called Marilyn. Once he'd sobered up again, he was quite shocked about what they'd done.'

'You haven't told us very much about what happened,' Ruth reminded him.

'Well, I wasn't there, now was I? Anything I tell you will only be repeating what they told me. Be better if you asked them yourselves.'

'John Moorhouse was the first man to be murdered,' Ruth told him quietly.

'Murdered!' Simon Gould looked startled. 'Are you saying that the four chaps alongside me in this picture are the four Benbury men who were murdered?'

'That's right.'

His eyes narrowed. 'And you came looking for me because you thought I might have been the one that *committed* those murders!'

'Well, naturally, it did cross our mind,' Paddy said blandly. Simon Gould looked at them in astonishment.

'I heard that! I've been listening to all you've been saying!'

All three of them turned to stare at Maggie Gould as she came into the room.

'And if my Simon's not the murderer – which he isn't, I can vouch for that because he's always here alongside me, day in, day out – then who is? Or,' she continued, her voice shaking, 'more to the point, is he going to be the next victim?'

'Hey, Maggie! What a thing to say!' Clumsily, Simon pulled her towards him, hugging her close to him in an attempt to reassure her.

'A couple of nights back you said you thought you saw that girl . . . that she'd stopped by for petrol . . .'

'Only said I *thought* it was her.'

'She could have been looking for you, Simon!'

'Nonsense!'

'She could have found out that you're living out this way and come looking for you,' she repeated stubbornly. 'You said yourself she said she was going one way, and then drove off in the other direction.'

'So what does that prove—?'

'Hold on a moment.' Ruth raised a hand to silence them both. 'Would you tell us what you know, Mrs Gould?'

Simon and Maggie exchanged looks, then Maggie took up the story.

'A couple of nights back, when my Simon came in for his supper, he said a woman had just stopped for petrol, and he thought he knew her by sight but couldn't remember her name. I thought it was one of the folks that have cottages round about and only come here in summer. He said he thought it was somebody else . . . someone he'd known at school. A girl called Maureen—'

'Did she say where she was going, Mr Gould?' interrupted Ruth.

Simon Gould nodded. 'She said she was on her way to see her folks who lived near Aberystwyth.' He rubbed a hand over his beard. 'The funny thing was she didn't even seem to know she was in Wales. She said she was from London way so she must have come all the way round through Gloucester. She said she didn't like motorways and she hadn't come on the M4 or M40. I told her which roads to take. Back through Brecon, then the A40 through Sennybridge to Llandovery—'

'Hold it!' Ruth cut him short. 'Did she take the route you suggested?'

'I doubt it. When she set off from here she was heading in the other direction towards Builth Wells!'

'Towards North Wales?'

He frowned. 'Yes, she could have been heading in that direction.'

Ruth nodded before turning to Paddy. 'Didn't one of Maureen Flynn's neighbours say that her parents lived in North Wales, and that she might have gone to visit them?'

'That's right. And they mentioned Llangollen.'

'And that plastic sack was found near Oswestry!'

Paddy nodded.

'Come on. We might be lucky. If she has gone to visit her parents in Llangollen then she still might be there.'

Simon Gould looked bewildered. 'Isn't there anything else you want to know?'

'Not at the moment. We will we back, probably.' Ruth handed him her card. 'If you should see Maureen Flynn again then ring this number.'

'I hope he doesn't see her again! His life might be in danger if he does,' Maggie stated aggressively. She was still clutching tightly to Simon's arm and shaking with shock.

'I don't think so,' Ruth assured her. 'You see, although your husband is in the picture he wasn't involved in the rape. The other four were, and that's probably why she killed them.'

'You mean for revenge? After all this time?'

'There's some things we never forget, Mrs Gould, no matter how hard we try. Something may have triggered off memories of what happened in that shed, reviving all the hate and revulsion she has kept hidden all these years.'

Maggie's dark eyes softened. 'Poor thing! It's just like what happens in some of them soaps I watch on the telly.'

TWENTY-FOUR

Detective Inspector Ruth Morgan and Detective Sergeant Paddy Hardcastle barely spoke to each other as they drove through the night towards Llangollen.

Ruth was fully occupied analysing the wealth of information they'd been given by Simon Gould. She felt even more convinced that her hunch about Maureen Flynn being their killer was the right one.

The outrage she must have felt for her anger to have remained active all these years – and then to have erupted, like some simmering volcano, bringing death and disruption to the lives of the four who had violated her all that time ago – was awesome.

Ruth could understand Maureen Flynn's desire for retribution, but why now, after all these years? What had happened? What was the catalyst that had set the sequence of events in motion?

She would have liked to talk about it, but she realized that Paddy needed all his concentration for driving. The rain, which had been an irritating fine mist when they'd left Simon Gould's garage at Pontydaren, had grown steadily heavier as they'd travelled north.

Dawn light was creeping over the Berwyn Mountains as they passed through the Tanan Valley, and she was able to catch a glimpse of the landscape skimming by on either side of them.

By the time they'd reached the outskirts of Llangollen the rain had stopped, and the ruin of Castell Dinas Bran, high on the conical hill overlooking the town, was clearly visible against the lightening skyline.

Paddy yawned. 'This is Llangollen,' he said as they crossed the ancient stone bridge that spanned the Dee and drove on into the town. 'All we have to do now is find the address Maureen Flynn's neighbour gave us.'

'That shouldn't be too difficult. It's not a very big place, and it's not busy at this time of the year. In summer, when they hold the National Eisteddfod, you can't move for people. Choirs from all over the world come here to participate.'

'A strange place to choose for retirement!'

'Oh, I don't know. It's very picturesque, and a good centre if you enjoy walking,' Ruth pointed out. 'If her father is into fishing then this stretch of the Dee is renowned for its salmon.'

They found the address they'd been given, Fifteen Druid's Rise, a neat semi on the fringe of the town, without any trouble at all.

'It looks as though she's here,' muttered Paddy as they pulled up outside and saw a red Ford Escort parked on the narrow gravel driveway.

'No, we're only assuming she is,' corrected Ruth, 'the same as we're only assuming that that is her car and that she did the murders.'

'It's bound to be her!' he said confidently. 'With what we know about her, and the information Simon Gould gave us, everything else falls into place, doesn't it?'

'I suppose so!'

Paddy gave her a quizzical look. 'You don't sound very confident,' he admonished.

'I've been thinking about it. If what Simon Gould told us is true then I can understand that she felt the need to be revenged, but why now, after all this time?'

Paddy stretched and yawned again. 'That's true! Something pretty traumatic must have happened to trigger off all those hidden memories after all these years.'

'Come on, there's only one way to find out.' Ruth undid her seat belt, checked her hair and make-up, and picked up her briefcase, which was lying on the back seat.

'Hold on! We know where the house is, so can't we go and have a coffee and something to eat first?'

'And come back to find she's made a getaway?'

Paddy peered at his watch. 'She won't be going anywhere at this hour of the morning! It's not eight o' clock. She'll still be in bed!'

'Then we'll be able to take her by surprise.'

'I think we ought to make contact with the local police and wait until they arrive,' Paddy advised.

Ruth shook her head. 'There's no need. When I phoned in from Pontydaren to let Superintendent Wilson know we intended coming straight here I asked the desk sergeant to phone the Llangollen police and request them to meet us at the Flynn's house.'

'And you gave them the address? Fifteen Druid's Rise, Llangollen? They probably don't come on duty until eight . . .'

'Then when they arrive to meet us they'll find we've already dealt with the matter and there's nothing for them to do.'

The door was opened by a thin upright man in his late sixties dressed in beige cord trousers, a brown and white striped shirt, and a brown cardigan. He was wearing felt slippers, and his grey hair was slicked to his skull as though he had just taken a bath or a shower.

'Mr Flynn?'

'Yes, but if you're selling anything we don't want it!' His probing eyes in his sharp face glinted suspiciously as they rested on Ruth's briefcase.

'No, we're not selling anything. We're police . . . plain clothes police.' Paddy flashed his identity card in front of Mr Flynn to confirm what he had said.

Mr Flynn frowned. 'So what do you want with me at this time of day?'

'Its not you exactly that we've called to see . . . It's your daughter, Maureen.'

'Jack, who on earth are you talking to at the door at this time in the morning?' A plump grey-haired woman in her mid-sixties, wearing a beige pleated skirt and a red knitted jumper, came into the hallway, peering over her husband's shoulder to see who was at the door.

'Mrs Flynn? We're police officers. Do you think we might come in?'

Reluctantly, Mr Flynn stood to one side and let Ruth and Paddy into the hallway.

'Now what's all this about?' asked Mrs Flynn. She looked flustered and was rubbing her rheumaticky hands together uneasily.

'We want to speak to your daughter, Maureen. She is here?'

'No, of course she isn't. She lives in Dutton; it's not far from London. I can give you her address.'

'We know where she lives, Mrs Flynn. We understood she had come up here to visit you?'

Mr Flynn shot a warning look at his wife. 'Who told you that?' he asked, speaking directly to Paddy.

'Her next door neighbour in Dutton thought so when we went to Windermere Mews looking for Maureen.'

'What on earth do you want to speak to her about that's so urgent that you had to come this early in the morning?' grumbled Mrs Flynn. 'We haven't had our breakfast yet!'

'I'm sorry about that, madam,' Paddy said stiffly. 'We have been driving all night.'

'So you're not the local police? So where have you come from then . . . if you've been driving all night?'

'We're from Benbury, madam.'

The word Benbury brought an instant transformation to both their faces. Mr Flynn's mouth became a tight line, and his eyes hardened. On Mrs Flynn's face was a look of fear.

'Now, if you would just answer one or two questions for us . . .'

'What sort of questions?' There was a sharp suspicious look in Mr Flynn's eyes.

'The red Ford Escort on the drive outside. Is that your daughter's car?'

'Of course it's not! What makes you ask that?'

'We understand she drives a red Escort.'

'She may well do, but it's not that one. That's mine. Bought it new at Llangollen Motors. Do you want to see the receipt?' he asked, his voice edged with annoyance.

'No, sir. We'll take your word for it.'

'Could you tell us when you last spoke to your daughter?' Ruth asked.

'What do you want to know that for?' A crafty look came into Mr Flynn's face.

Ruth turned to his wife. 'Mrs Flynn, we need to speak to Maureen urgently. It's a confidential matter. We know she has left home, and we have been led to believe that she was coming to visit you.'

'Well, she hasn't. She phoned yesterday to say she was going to come and see us, but when we said we were going away for a few days she said in that case it might be a while before we saw her, because she might be going abroad, but that she'd be in touch—' Mrs Flynn stopped and clamped a hand over her mouth. The fear was back in her eyes as she looked across at her husband.

His face was thunderous, but he remained tight-lipped.

'Perhaps you can tell me where she has gone, Mr Flynn?'

'Abroad, like my wife said.'

'She didn't exactly tell you where she was going on holiday?'

'No! She's probably going there to work. She does this research for people,' gabbled Mrs Flynn. 'She's been working for some professor or the other for some months now. Something to do with the Far East. So, that's probably where she's going.'

Ruth nodded as though she accepted what the older woman was saying.

'Is that all?' snapped Mr Flynn. 'We've told you all we know.'

'Yes, that will be fine, thank you!' Ruth smiled. 'I'll leave a phone number, and I'd be grateful if you would let us know when your daughter next gets in touch with you.'

He scowled. 'What is it you need to see her about that is so urgent?'

'It's to do with something in Benbury, sir,' Paddy informed him.

Again the two older people exchanged looks. This time there was a definite warning in Mr Flynn's eyes as they met his wife's quizzical glance.

'It's about the murders that have taken place in Benbury over the past few weeks,' Ruth added. She reached into her briefcase, and brought out the photograph of Maureen and the five boys. 'Do you remember this being taken when your daughter passed her A-levels?' she asked as she handed it to Mrs Flynn.

Mrs Flynn blanched. Her hand shook as she took the photograph. Silently, she held it out to her husband. He took it from her and stared at it belligerently.

'What about it?' he demanded.

'You probably already know from the newspapers, and from the news bulletins on radio and television, that four of the men in that photograph have been murdered,' Ruth told him. 'John Moorhouse, Sandy Franklin, Brian Patterson and Dennis Jackson.'

He gave it a perfunctory glance. 'What about it?' he repeated, harshly.

'We have been trying to trace the remaining two people . . . Simon Gould, and your daughter, Maureen.'

Mr Flynn shrugged his thin shoulders. 'She's not here. We've already told you that.'

'She may be in danger.'

Again there was an exchange of glances between Mr and Mr Flynn. Mrs Flynn relaxed slightly, but she didn't speak.

'We have heard about what happened on the day the six of them passed their A-levels,' pursued Ruth.

The tension was too much for Mrs Flynn. Sobbing, she buried her face in her hands. 'I'm glad they're dead,' she exclaimed in a muffled voice. 'It's justice at last.'

'They ruined Maureen's life . . . and ours,' Mr Flynn stated angrily. 'It might be why she wants to go abroad, to get away from all the gossip. Now she'll be an exile the same as us. We don't belong up here. Ever since we've been in Llangollen we've longed to get back to Benbury . . . Now none of us will ever be able to go back there.'

Ruth looked at him questioningly, waiting for him to say more, to tell them what he knew about his daughter's involvement with the Benbury murders, but he remained silent.

'We'll let ourselves out,' she said at last, breaking the interminable silence. 'You will remember to let us know as soon as you hear from Maureen? It's very important that you do.'

Maureen Flynn, sitting in her car on the outskirts of Llangollen, felt an overwhelming sense of rejection as she switched off her mobile phone. Her parents had told her it wasn't convenient for her to visit them at the moment because they were going away for a few days.

Going away for a few days, were they? And they couldn't even be bothered to ask why she wanted to see them. Not even when she had hinted that if she couldn't visit them now she wouldn't be coming to see them for quite some time because she was planning to go to the Far East on a working holiday.

Their lifestyle and their plans always came first, she thought resentfully, and she was expected to fit her life in accordingly. It had been the same when she'd been raped – her parents had been more concerned about how it affected them, and what friends and neighbours would say if they ever found out what had happened, than they were about how she felt.

As her feeling of resentment subsided, Maureen began to reason out what she must do next. Obviously, it was risky to stay in either England or Wales now that the police were looking for her, and although the picture they had flashed up on the telly looked nothing at all like her, someone might recognize her name and connect her with what had happened.

There was no doubt about it, she told herself: the right thing to do was to return to Dutton, pack up her personal belongings and vacate her flat. Where she went after that was equally important. Would she be safe on the Continent, she wondered. Not France or Belgium, of course, since these days they were merely an extension of Britain; so, she would need to go further afield. She fancied Spain, or Portugal, with their warm sunshine and relaxed lifestyles, but again she wondered if that wasn't far too risky because it was too much on the doorstep for safety.

She didn't want to go to Africa or India. Too hot for one thing, and then there was the language barrier. She didn't want to draw attention to herself by having to seek out people who spoke English. And another thing! She'd need to earn a living, so she would have to go somewhere where English was the standard language. Which left Australia, New Zealand, America or Canada, and none of them appealed to her. South America was a possibility, of course, and would be an extremely safe haven, but would she be able to find work there?

Her thoughts drifted. Why on earth had she phoned her parents? It wasn't as though they were expecting her to visit them or that they would think it odd if they didn't hear from her for a few months. And why tell them that she was off to the Far East on a working holiday with Professor Harmer?

'Make sure you see something of the place while you are out there,' her father advised.

'And don't work too hard. Remember it is supposed to be a holiday,' her mother had added. 'Don't let that boss of yours take advantage of you.'

There was little likelihood of that happening, Maureen thought cynically as she recalled her mother's words.

She hadn't really intended going to the Far East, of course, but thinking about it, she quite liked the idea of trailing Phillip Harmer without his knowledge. There was plenty of time to finalize the details. All the time in the world, in fact, since the flight would be a long one. She could spend the travelling time fine-tuning her plans and deciding whether she'd contact him in advance to let him know that she was following him, or simply let it be the very last thing he would ever know.

Excitedly, she slammed her foot hard down on the accelerator, and then had to brake suddenly as a sudden sharp bend took her by surprise. Her car skidded, and it left her frightened and shaking, her pulse racing. An accident was the last thing she wanted to be involved in, so speed was out of the question on these minor roads, she decided. She'd head for the motorway, then she could really put her foot down.

It had been madness coming to Wales. Visiting her parents was the last thing she should do at the moment. If they knew the truth about what she had done they wouldn't be prepared to help her sort things out, any more than they'd been all those years ago.

Her father's rancour had destroyed them as a family, she reflected, and even now, all these years later, his manner still managed to convey his distaste and disapproval, as if what had happened had been her fault. He'd never been prepared to acknowledge that she'd tried to stop them but had been powerless to do so, and that all her efforts had been completely ineffectual.

The fact that she had gone into a pub with those boys had been her downfall, in every sense of the word. Her father's upbringing had been so strict and puritanical that in his eyes, now as well as then, her action was quite unforgivable. That was what damned her in his eyes. Probably it had been the main reason why he had refused to inform the police about what had happened.

Well, nothing could change him now. He was a bigoted old man, set in his ways. He was responsible for all the frustrations she'd felt ever since, but she also blamed her mother. If her mother had stood up to him, made it clear that what happened wasn't her fault, comforted her, taken her side, and helped to present a united front against his bigotry, she might have been able to forget it ever happened, Maureen thought angrily.

For almost fifteen years she had managed to shut away the memories and get on with her life. To outsiders, it might have appeared to be a narrow, self-contained, sterile existence, but it had been one which satisfied her. That was until she had met Phillip Harmer.

Phillip Harmer had been the fuse that had ignited the trail of bitter revenge. A man who was as bigoted and critical as her father. He had picked at the scab and ripped open the deep-seated wound until it had haemorrhaged.

Retaliation had been sweet, but now she would have to pay for that luxury. First, though, why not make him share the retribution?

Once she'd punished him, in the same way as she had the others who'd been responsible for her misery, then she didn't care what happened. She wasn't even planning any further ahead than that. All she wanted to do was make sure she achieved this ultimate goal before she was intercepted by the police.

TWENTY-FIVE

A s she headed towards the M4 Motorway at Chepstow, Maureen's spirits lightened and she decided to take a quick break. Once she was on the motorway she could move into the fast lane, forget the speed limit, put her foot down and speed non-stop to Maidenhead.

As she sat waiting for her coffee to cool, she took out a pad and pen and began writing a letter to Phillip Harmer. She wanted him to know every morbid detail of what had happened since he'd last seen her.

She smiled to herself; she'd post it right away, then he would receive it before his body was found. They would think he had committed suicide because he felt such deep remorse for treating her in such a callous way.

'Superintendent Wilson is going to crucify us when he hears what's happened,' groaned Paddy as they got back into their car outside Fifteen Druid's Rise.

'Yes! We should have checked out the licence plate and confirmed with Swansea that it was her car before we presumed that it was,' Ruth stated crisply.

'OK. That was my fault,' Paddy agreed contritely. 'I admit I leaped to conclusions. I blame it on being so tired and so hungry that I wasn't thinking straight.'

'If you're still hungry, then perhaps we'd better do something about it before we head south again. There should be a cafe of some sort open in the town by now.'

'Or we could report to the local station, and make use of their canteen,' he suggested.

'No, I've a much better idea. We've earned a decent breakfast, and some real coffee, and the chance to sort out our story before we visit them, so why not find a hotel, and treat ourselves to a slap-up breakfast?'

Paddy grinned. 'And we can spend the entire drive back to

Benbury deciding how we are going to explain to Superintendent Wilson that our suspect has gone off on a working holiday to Hong Kong, or Bangkok, or somewhere in the Far East.'

'We certainly won't get the chance to go out there after her,' said Ruth with a sigh.

'No, I'm afraid not,' agreed Paddy. 'We'll be expected to hand over the case to Interpol, and let them take all the credit for our hard work. That's if they finally manage to track her down.'

'I rather think they will,' mused Ruth.

'Oh? Why do you say that?'

'I don't think she's quite finished killing yet.'

Paddy frowned. 'Simon Gould said he wasn't involved in any way with the rape . . .'

'No, not Simon Gould. I don't think she's in the slightest bit interested in him. No, I was thinking of the person who must have triggered this off.'

'I don't think I'm following your line of reasoning?'

'It's sixteen years since she was raped. In all that time she has never made any kind of retaliation. Then, out of the blue, she suddenly hunts down, and kills, the four boys who had raped her . . .'

'And ruined her life and her parents' lives.'

'Exactly! So why has she waited sixteen years?'

Paddy shook his head. 'I don't know . . . but I bet you're going to tell me.'

'I think it was because the memory of what happened all those years ago was suddenly revived.'

'You think she might have been raped again?'

Ruth shook her head. 'No, not exactly raped, but something equally traumatic, so that it has brought those hidden memories, which have been bottled up for so long, bubbling to the surface.'

'You make it sound as though she's mentally deranged. If that's the case then why not simply kill the person who did that?'

Ruth nodded in agreement. 'That's what I think she may be planning – hence her trip to the Far East.'

'You mean her recent employer, Professor Harmer, may have something to do with this?'

'That's right. Let's hope Interpol act fast. She's already killed four times so, as far as she is concerned, what does once more matter?'

Detective Inspector Ruth Morgan and Detective Sergeant Paddy Hardcastle were travelling westwards on the M4 when the message came through of a major crash only fifteen miles ahead of them.

'A red Ford Escort, travelling at an excessively high speed, has crashed through the central barrier and ploughed into the path of an oncoming tanker. The driver of the Escort, a woman, died instantly. Ten other vehicles have been involved in the collision but there are no other serious injuries, apart from the driver of the tanker, who has been taken to Wexham Park Hospital suffering from shock and leg injuries.'

Paddy and Ruth exchanged glances. 'A red Ford Escort?'

'Travelling at high speed towards London!'

'I'll check out if they have identified the driver yet,' Ruth said. 'I think we can safely bet, though, that it's our suspect, Maureen Flynn.'

'Tell them that we're on our way and that we'll be there in less than ten minutes,' Paddy ordered as he reached out with one hand and fixed the blue warning light on the top of their car and switched on the siren.

As they pulled up at the scene of the crash, Ruth leaped out of the car and hurried over to the wrecked Ford Escort. By the time Paddy joined her, she had confirmed that it was indeed Maureen Flynn.

'May I?' she asked, looking askance at the officer in charge as she reached out for Maureen's handbag, which was lying in the wrecked car alongside her.

She pulled out Maureen's driver's licence and passed it triumphantly to Paddy, then she took out the letter which was also in the handbag and frowned as she saw that it was addressed to Professor Harmer.

'Go ahead and open it,' Paddy ordered crisply when she looked at him hesitantly.

As she read Maureen's catalogue of admissions, Ruth let out a low whistle. 'This amounts to a confession,' she pronounced. 'It most certainly winds up the case against her.'

'Quite a satisfactory conclusion to your first investigation since your appointment to Benbury, but at least there'll be no need for a referral to Interpol,' Paddy said with a degree of smugness.

'No, nor will there be any need to alert Professor Phillip Harmer that he was likely to be Maureen Flynn's next target,' added Ruth.